DEATH PENALTY

Deep under the main stand, far down the pla[...]
tunnel, [w]ere the dressing-rooms. At the far end of
home te[a]m's dressing-room steaming water rose slo[...]
to the r[i]m of the communal bath. Dim echoes of [...]
crowd's [ro]ars filtering down did not disturb the conce[n-]
tration of the dark, poised figure crouched and waitin[g]
behind a [l]ocker . . .

POINT CRIME

DEATH PENALTY

Dennis Hamley

Cover illustration by David Wyatt

■SCHOLASTIC

Scholastic Children's Books,
Scholastic Publications Ltd,
7-9 Pratt Street, London NW1 0AE, UK

Scholastic Inc.,
555 Broadway, New York, NY 10012-3999, USA

Scholastic Canada Ltd,
123 Newkirk Road, Richmond Hill,
Ontario, Canada L4C 3G5

Ashton Scholastic Pty Ltd,
P O Box 579, Gosford, New South Wales,
Australia

Ashton Scholastic Ltd,
Private Bag 92801, Penrose, Auckland,
New Zealand

First published in the UK by Scholastic Publications Ltd, 1994

Text copyright © Dennis Hamley, 1994

Cover illustration copyright © David Wyatt, 1994

ISBN 0 590 55705 X

Typeset by TW Typesetting, Midsomer Norton, Avon
Printed by Cox & Wyman Ltd, Reading, Berks

10 9 8 7 6 5 4 3 2 1

For Corry and Graham
who knew the way to Wembley.

My grateful thanks go to Mike Sparrow
and all the Wembley staff
who put me right when I got there.

THE ALL-STAR FOOTBALL YEARBOOK

PART 8

CLUBS OF THE PREMIERSHIP AND FOOTBALL LEAGUE

League Division One

Club	RADWICK RANGERS
Ground	LOURING PARK, RADWICK
Colours	Cherry red shirts with yellow trim, cherry red shorts, red socks with yellow tops. *Away strip:* Royal blue shirts, shorts and socks.
Nickname	Rangers
Ground record	53,687 v. Tottenham Hotspur. FA Cup 6th Round, 1957
Chairman	Walter Blyton, OBE
Secretary	John L Forbes AISA
Manager	George Maxton
Coach	Wally Kerns
Goalkeepers:	Chris Kingdon
	Ted Rankin
	Archie Wilkes
Defenders:	Willie Banks
	Arthur Burden
	Greg Perkins

	Dave Prendergast
	Geoff Rundle
	Winston Somerset
	Len Symes
Midfield:	Lee Boatman
	Stu Burton
	Ossie Canklow
	Fred Dale
	Gus Fame
	Darren King
	Colin Thresher
Forwards:	Steve Craig
	Declan Flynn
	Rick McBain
	Ade Ojokwe
	Ronnie Raikes
	Kevin Ray
	Doug Wadsworth
	Nicky Worrall
	Gary Young
Honours:	**Champions** Div 3 North 1928:
	Champions Div 2 1935
	Champions Div 1 1949, 1953, 1960
	FA Cup Winners 1937, 1956, 1963
	League Cup Winners 1968

Prologue

Little boys of three should not see such sights.

The morning was sunny and warm and he had just finished his breakfast. Mummy said he must play in the garden. So he took his Mickey Mouse tricycle from its place in the back porch and rode it up the garden path to where the big copper beech tree shaded the lawn.

There he looked up, puzzled. A pair of white training shoes swung to and fro in front of his face. His gaze travelled upwards. He saw socks, blue tracksuit bottoms, a white sweatshirt. They clothed a body. He looked higher still.

A face, its eyes still open, stared down at him. A rope, one end tied to a thick branch, was round the neck.

Body and boy faced each other for a few moments.

"Daddy?" the boy asked tentatively.

No answer.

The boy turned his Mickey Mouse tricycle round and half-pedalled, half-ran back up the path.

"Mummy!" he called.

A strikingly beautiful woman with long blonde hair and the confident movements of an athlete emerged from the kitchen.

"Daddy's up the tree and he won't come down," said the boy.

The woman ran up the path. She saw her husband. There was no scream from her, just a sharp intake of breath. She stood stock still for a full minute, looking upwards.

Then she bent down, put her arms round the little boy and whispered in his ear words which hissed like jets into his brain and stayed there until he understood them and their meaning gave purpose to his whole life.

"I know who's to blame for this. And he will pay. Oh, yes, my son, you and I will make him pay."

1

Twenty thousand fans thronged Louring Park. Radwick Rangers, top of the First Division and leading by eight points, were playing Leicester City. The April sun picked out Leicester's blue shirts and white shorts and Radwick's cherry red shirts with the three big yellow chevrons, red shorts and yellow-topped red socks as the players' movements made patterns over the still-startling green of a well-kept pitch.

Annabel Ferris was not one of the twenty thousand. Seventeen last Tuesday and possessor of seven GCSEs (one of which – in Business Studies – had got her a job in the office at Radwick Rangers under the eye of the formidable Miss Gibson), she was in town looking at the shops with her best friend Karen James. Radwick Rangers might pay her wages, but she didn't have to *like* the game they played – just one of the people who played it.

As she and Karen examined a skirt in Next, she pondered on the paradox. People who went to football matches needed their heads examined and professional footballers were *thick*, yet more and more she found herself thinking about Stu Burton. She also felt annoyed that at that moment he was probably playing his heart out for Radwick Rangers and not thinking about her at all.

Deep under the main stand, far down the players' tunnel, were the dressing-rooms. At the far end of the home team's dressing-room steaming water rose slowly to the rim of the communal bath. Dim echoes of the crowd's roars filtering down did not disturb the concentration of the dark, poised figure crouched and waiting behind a locker . . .

For once, things were not going Radwick's way. Surely they weren't heading for their first home defeat of the season? Half-time had come and gone: Leicester were one up.

And now Leicester's number 9, a striker nearly as lethal as Radwick's own Kevin Ray, had broken free. Ted Rankin in goal seemed to hesitate before rushing out to narrow the angle; while Geoff Rundle, defender way out of position, charged desperately across the penalty area.

Rundle reached the Leicester striker and took off in a wild feet-first charge which scythed his legs from under him. The referee blew his whistle and bustled up. Without hesitation he produced the red card and waved it in the Radwick player's face.

No arguments. The crudest of professional fouls. Not even the most fanatic Radwick supporter could complain.

Geoff Rundle trudged to the dugout, where Wally Kerns, the trainer, waited in his red tracksuit.

"Tough, lad," he said.

"I'm having an early bath," replied Geoff.

"That's what they all say."

The burly, forbidding figure of George Maxton, the manager, now filled Geoff's vision. In his smart grey suit he had come down from the directors' box; no tracksuit during matches for him.

"That was a *stupid* thing to do and you'll pay for it. We've lost you for the most important part of the season."

The voice was low: the anger bit into Geoff's brain. The square Scots face with the hard blue eyes and down-turned mouth struck fear into him – he already knew that he faced a lengthy suspension which could be disastrous on top of all the other injury worries.

"Sorry, boss," he muttered and stumbled up the tunnel towards the dressing-rooms.

George Maxton turned to Wally.

"Change of plan," he said. "Don't substitute Raikes now. Keep him on. I don't care how tired he gets: he's our best hope."

"Best hope of what?" said Wally.

The penalty had been taken: Leicester had scored and were two up with fifteen minutes to go.

Stuart Burton, known to his mates as Stu, was at seventeen the youngest player ever to pull on a Radwick first-team shirt. After Leicester's second goal, all the elation of this his first senior game evaporated. Surely his arrival didn't mean the start of a rot? Nothing could stop Radwick going up to the Premiership, could it?

Well, there had been too many injuries for a start. That was why he was in the first team squad so soon, the envy of his mates Rick, Doug and Gus, with whom he lived in Connie Wilshaw's club lodging house. It was also the reason why David Prendergast had been bought for a huge fee just before the transfer deadline: another debut day. He glanced towards Dave, who looked back and spread his hands in an "It's nothing to do with me" gesture.

But we'll be blamed if we lose, thought Stu grimly. He tried to put the idea out of his head and think of Annabel instead and where he'd take her that evening.

* * *

4

Ronnie Raikes knew what the signal from the dug-out would be long before it came. The plan was that he would be substituted fifteen minutes from the end, to save his poor, buckling thirty-seven-year-old legs for a few more games. Radwick were by now supposed to be comfortably in the lead.

But two down, with ten men – well, he'd have to stay on the field and work a bit of magic. He understood that, but he didn't have to like it.

No, don't be ungrateful. Last August, a great career seemed finally over. With forty England caps, the finest forward of his age, his career had reached its zenith in Europe and then dwindled down the divisions back home until Northampton Town, of all people, were giving him a free transfer.

Then a phonecall and a familiar Glaswegian voice he'd never thought to hear again – George Maxton.

"Ronnie? I want you here at Radwick. You can do a job for me."

"But, George, I'm finished. I'm on the scrap-heap."

"Not you, Ronnie. Genius never dies. I've got just the partner for you."

So Ronnie arrived at Radwick for his marvellous Indian summer. He was given the captain's arm-band and found himself playing alongside the brilliant young Kevin Ray.

I make the bullets and he fires them, thought

Ronnie, and so far this season that had worked thirty-five times.

The figure in the dressing-room waited for the sound of footsteps in the corridor. Rubber-gloved fingers gripped the blade of a long, razor-sharp knife. Adrenalin coursed round the arched, lithe body. Keen eyes peered round the side of the locker.

The unsuspecting Geoff Rundle, his back to the intruder, stood at the side of the steaming bath. He never jumped in: he never even tried his toe in the water. He must have heard for a split second the snarling whistle of the knife's journey through the air. He was dead before he hit the water.

The figure looked at the body lying face-down in the water and darted away.

If Geoff Rundle still had ears to hear, he would have heard the faint echo of the crowd's roar as Radwick Rangers pulled a goal back.

Ronnie had done it, of course. He received the ball from Ade Ojokwe and made a superb twenty-yard pass, splitting the defence for Kevin to latch on to and score his thirty-sixth of the season.

They hugged each other ritually, then Kevin said, "It's a shame they're substituting you. If you stayed we could have three more."

"I *am* staying on," said Ronnie. "Wally says so."

Kevin didn't answer but got on with the game.

There were no more goals and Radwick had lost.

George Maxton didn't join the players directly after the match. He stood in the boardroom talking to Walter Blyton, Radwick's chairman, who had poured thousands of his own money into the club.

"Bit of a setback today, then, George?" said Blyton.

"We'll not fail," said George Maxton. "I've staked my reputation on putting Radwick in the Premier League."

"You'd better," said Blyton. "You're finished here if you don't. This club means too much to the people of this town. They've waited too long."

A dowdy tea-lady in a brown uniform dress edged with white piping slipped to Blyton's side and handed him a full cup.

"Two lumps, Mr Blyton," she murmured. "Just as you like it."

"Thank you, Mrs Grundy," said Blyton.

The tea-lady disappeared into the throng.

"There," said Blyton. "That's a perfect example of what I mean. The loyalty of people round here is *fantastic*. Do you know how that woman came to work for us?"

Far from not knowing, Maxton wished Radwick had scored a goal for every time he had heard it.

"Well, I'll tell you. Last year she knocked on the door of my house. There she was, our Mrs

Grundy, clutching a silver urn. And do you know what was in that urn?"

"No," said Maxton, lying through his teeth.

"The ashes of her husband. That man had stood on the North Terrace every home game for forty years. And he'd caught pneumonia there. I'm not trying to be funny when I say he *died* for the club. She told me his dearest wish was to have his ashes scattered over the pitch. Well, of course I agreed. A fine memorial to Jim Grundy, a faithful supporter. *And* I gave her a job at the club."

I'm glad about the job, thought George Maxton, though a better memorial to Jim Grundy would have been a roof over the North Terrace. But he said nothing. Besides, the North Terrace would soon be no more when the bulldozers came in and a new all-seater stand took its place.

"*That's* the sort of faith and devotion you've got to satisfy," said Blyton. "The Mrs Grundys of this world and their husbands."

"We'll not fail," repeated Maxton.

"City won," someone called from across the room. "Three-nil away to Notts County."

"We'll get there," said Maxton. "We're still five points ahead."

George Maxton had no idea that far below him the bath was ringed with horrified players looking at a body with a blade planted between its shoulder-blades, floating in water cloudy with blood.

Kevin Ray's face was chalk-white.

"It's Geoff," he muttered. "Why Geoff?"

Ronnie put a hand on his shoulder.

"Get a grip, lad," he said.

Ade Ojokwe stood silent, his hands clenching and unclenching at his sides.

Ted Rankin leant against the wall.

"They'll blame me for it," he moaned. "Oh, God, they'll blame me."

Wally Kerns had already rushed out to phone the police and tell the world.

Stu was over his first shock. He had taken his eyes away from the body and was surveying the players, watching and thinking.

2

Inspector Wagstaffe was not a football fan, and he warned all the detective sergeants and constables in his team that, for the duration of this investigation, neither were they. If the outcome was a lifetime in the nick for some childhood hero, then so be it.

When he arrived at the ground with Sergeant Cumberland and the forensic team, the scene in the dressing-room was exactly the same except that the water in the bath was redder. Nobody had touched the body: nobody wanted to, anyway. George Maxton had charged down the tunnel, roaring, "Everyone stays where they are!" Nobody felt inclined to disobey.

But when the first shock was over, the questions started. Stu was first.

"Why should they blame you, Ted?" he said.

The goalkeeper had got over his anguish.

"No reason," he said lamely.

"Yes there is," said Ossie Canklow. "You two had a blinding row after training on Tuesday. I heard you. You said 'I'll kill you, Rundle!'"

"It was a joke," muttered Ted.

"If that was a joke I hope I'm a long way off when you're serious," said Ossie.

Little sharp-eyed Nicky Worrall spoke. He was standing next to Ade Ojokwe, whose hands still clenched and unclenched.

"You won't be sorry he's gone, will you, Ade?" he said maliciously. "He was always on at you."

"Rundle was a racist," said Dave Prendergast. "I've only been here a fortnight and I could see that a mile off."

Ade's voice was quiet but there was anger behind it.

"He was not good to me," he said, "but I can look after myself."

"I bet you can," said Nicky.

Ade shot him a furious look. "I wouldn't want him dead, man," he shouted.

"He knew who to pick on," rumbled the huge Winston Somerset in his deep voice. "He wouldn't dare say 'boo' to me."

"Just a minute," said Stu. "This is daft. None of

us could have had anything to do with it. We were all out on the pitch."

"Nicky wasn't," said Kevin Ray. "Neither was Lee. You were substitutes. I expected Lee on for Ronnie before Geoff got sent off."

"Yeah," said Lee Boatman. "The boss told me to warm up ready and then I never got on the field."

"What about you, Nicky?" said Kevin.

"I was sitting there all the time. Behind the boss and Wally. I was expecting the nod to go on. I never moved."

"Who says?" jeered Ossie Canklow.

"*I* say!" roared Nicky as belligerently as his high-pitched voice would allow. His wiry body quivered with sudden temper and instinctively he put his fists up to fight.

Ronnie Raikes spoke for the first time.

"Cool it, all of you," he said. "Save it all for the police. We'll do no good to ourselves like this."

There was immediate quiet. Ronnie was respected. Of medium height, with thick hair starting to grey and deepset eyes looking out of a weather-beaten face, he was every inch the old international.

"They'll be here in a minute," he said. "They'll swarm all over the place. They'll talk to us one by one. And when they do, *nobody* puts a finger on anyone else. There'll be no talk about blazing rows, racist taunts or where the substitutes were when the match was on. Just show them that you could have

12

had nothing to do with it, and when they ask what you thought about Geoff, say he was a good team-mate but you didn't know much about his private life. Because most of the time he was, and I for one didn't."

The atmosphere calmed considerably.

"Well said, Ronnie," said Kevin.

"Everyone has rows," muttered Ossie Canklow to Ted.

"Forget it," replied Ted.

"Sorry, mate," said Nicky to Ade.

Ade ruffled the little winger's hair. "I bet you never left the bench," he said.

There was a sudden clatter outside. George Maxton was leading in Inspector Wagstaffe and his team.

Inspector Wagstaffe and Sergeant Cumberland finally finished their interviews at eleven that night. Everyone who had access to the dressing-room – manager, directors, coach, players, staff – made simple statements about where they were and their relationship to Geoff Rundle. The murder had taken place during the second half. They were all either playing or watching and they all had several thousand witnesses. Inspector Wagstaffe had used the chairman's room for his interviews, Sergeant Cumberland the manager's office. When the last interviewees had been released they met in the boardroom, where Walter Blyton was waiting for them.

"You're off duty now," he said. "I'll pour you each a drink and leave you to talk in peace."

Inspector Wagstaffe settled back in an armchair. Through the large window he could see the brooding bulk of stands and terraces. The pitch was an enigmatic stretch of grey in the faint moonlight. The inspector sighed.

"We have a player sent off, so fed up and angry that he won't watch the rest of the game. He goes to have a bath and get changed early. He's murdered with a knife which forensic believe, and the post mortem will probably confirm, was thrown."

"So we have an invisible, psychic knife-thrower who *knew* Geoff Rundle was going to be sent off," said Sergeant Cumberland.

"Either that or it was a random killing."

"What sort of psychopath goes to all that trouble to do a random killing?"

The inspector sighed again.

"What did you make of the players?" he said.

"I got what you might call a united front," said Cumberland. "And you have to admit they have the most perfect, cast-iron alibis in the history of crime. What did the men you spoke to think about Rundle?"

"The best friend anyone could have had. Epitome of British sporting virtue."

"Same here. You'd think being sent off for committing a particularly vicious foul qualified him for the Nobel Peace Prize."

Inspector Wagstaffe took a long swallow of his whisky.

"I reckon," he said, "that this one's going to be a long trail a-winding."

The players were interviewed alphabetically, so Stu got away early. He was still in his Rangers strip: he hadn't even taken his boots off. He had answered the inspector's questions carefully and clearly, had watched his shrewd grey eyes surveying him and noted the thinning hair and long, nicotine-stained fingers. This man worries too much, thought Stu. He needs to lighten up.

As he came out of the chairman's office and Ossie took his place they touched hands briefly, like a substitute acknowledging the player whose place he is taking.

"No worries," Stu had muttered.

"Great," Ossie had replied.

Then Stu had clattered down passages and stairs back to the dressing-room. Thankfully the body had been removed and the bath drained, but police were everywhere, measuring, peering and dusting everything for fingerprints.

A uniformed sergeant stood at the door as he entered.

"Name?"

"Stuart Burton."

"Been interviewed yet?"

"Yes."

"You can use the visitors' dressing-room. They've gone. Go in and get your clothes first."

Stu went in and collected them from his locker. As he left, the sergeant stopped him again.

"Right, let's go through these."

Stu shoved jeans, socks, shirt and the rest at him. The sergeant searched the pockets carefully. Stu knew there would be nothing incriminating: he hoped to God there was nothing embarrassing.

There wasn't. The sergeant was satisfied. His manner changed. He smiled.

"Good on you, lad," he said. "You played a blinder today."

"I was rubbish," said Stu.

"Not from where I was standing. We don't just watch the crowd, you know."

Stu felt an unexpected relief as he drove his Peugeot 106 out of the players' carpark. He was proud of his little car, bought with the first fruits of his new contract just two days after he'd passed his driving test. He was aware of reporters and television cameras massing outside the ground as he headed towards the lodging house. Stu was new to Radwick and lived with other young players in the clubhouse run by the energetic Connie

Wilshaw, fanatical Rangers supporter. She looked after them – as she had generations of Radwick players – with possessive zeal. Stu's great mates were there: Rick McBain from Edinburgh, Doug Wadsworth of Runcorn, and Gus Fame, of the Rastafarian locks, from Brixton. And still they were in the Youth team, with occasional forays into the reserves. But their turn would come – sooner perhaps, Stu thought, than they bargained for, the way things were going.

He stopped at red traffic lights, signalling left for the lodging house. Then he looked at his watch, winced, and turned right for Annabel's house instead.

Yes, he really fancied Annabel. She was small, with red-gold hair and blue eyes, could look fabulous when she wanted, and certainly wasn't one of the daft and desperate football groupies he'd already encountered and vowed to keep clear of.

It was a pity she wasn't too pleased with him as they headed back into town.

"I can't help being late," he said. "It's not every day one of your back four ends up with a knife in his ribs."

"Don't drive so fast," she answered.

It's going to be a lousy evening, Stu thought.

But he was wrong. Annabel's mood changed completely once they were in the Star of India, munching poppadoms and looking at menus in the comfortable half-darkness. She let Stu babble on about what was obviously most on his mind. The series of confrontations in the dressing-room was nagging away inside his brain.

"That Geoff wasn't exactly the greatest person who ever lived," he said. "A few people had it in for him."

"Don't speak ill of the dead," said Annabel.

"He can't hear," Stu replied. "Besides, it's true. Ted and Ade were obviously scared stiff when they saw his body, and it wasn't just shock."

"Ade's lovely," said Annabel. "Nicest player in the squad. He often comes down into the office. So does Ted, but he's always complaining."

Annabel worked in the small typing and clerical pool presided over by Miss Gibson, personal assistant to the club secretary John Forbes. Apart from the regular passing through (whenever Miss Gibson's gaze could be avoided) of young male faces already slightly familiar from newspapers and television, it was a typical open-plan office.

"Ted and Geoff had been having a rumble for weeks – I don't know what it was about. And Ossie was right. They had a real bust-up last Thursday after training. Wally and Ronnie had to pull them apart."

"How can that have anything to do with it?" said Annabel. "Ted was on the field with you."

"He could have got somebody else to do it. Paid him, perhaps."

"Whatever sort of people do you footballers mix with?" said Annabel.

"And Ade," Stu went on. "Geoff often had a go at him. It was sickening sometimes. National Front stuff. Yet he never said a word to Winston."

"And what did you do about it?"

"Well, I told him to shut up once or twice. Most of the lads pretended it didn't happen. But Geoff was clever. He knew when to needle and when not. George and Wally had no inkling it ever happened. Ade was too proud to say anything. But I wouldn't have blamed Ade if he'd slipped a knife in Geoff's ribs."

"But Ade was *playing*," said Annabel. "And how could anyone know Geoff would be in the dressing-room early?"

Stu shook his head.

"You go round in circles on this," he said. "My head's aching."

"Leave it to the police," said Annabel.

"All right," said Stu. "But just think: there's a killer loose in the place where we both work, and who knows it won't happen again?"

"It could be you next," said Annabel.

"It could be *you*."

They fell silent for some minutes and ate thoughtfully. Then, as the last of her curry disappeared from her plate, Annabel said, "Forget it. We're too young to die."

So they tried to forget it and have a great night out at a club. Stu managed to blank out the vision of Geoff's body lying face-down in slowly reddening water. Only when they drove past Louring Park in the small hours and saw the gaunt, grim outline of the stands with the floodlights standing on guard at each corner like scarecrow skeletons did it return. Then Annabel and Stu squeezed hands and shivered at the thought of what might still be stalking the darkness inside.

3

Rangers' training ground was five kilometres out of town, tree-lined and springy-turfed with a large brick pavilion housing changing-rooms and clubhouse. It was a subdued bunch of players who met there on Monday morning.

George Maxton was waiting for them. Today he wore a tracksuit. Even though he had been a successful – some would say a great – player, the grey suit he had worn on Saturday somehow sat easier on him.

Before training started, George made the team stand in a semi-circle round him. He and Wally Kerns surveyed them.

"Right," barked George. "Back to business. We've had a shock but we'll put it behind us. Let the police do the worrying. That's what they're paid for. We've got a title and promotion to win."

The players shuffled from foot to foot and looked at George uneasily.

"And we won't do it the way you played on Saturday. You were *slack*. You've got to be *sharp*. When you're up there with the Liverpools and the Arsenals, the Blackburns and the Man Uniteds, you'll be torn to pieces."

Heads went down. Eyes surveyed blades of grass and insteps of boots.

"But you *can* match them. You're good. I chose you myself to do a job. Everyone is here because *I* said so and I don't make mistakes about what players can do on the field."

Heads were raised again and smiles appeared on faces. The atmosphere lightened. George Maxton was a shrewd motivator.

"Here's where we went wrong on Saturday. The rot set in after their first goal. And that, Ted Rankin, was down to you. You *catch* crosses, you don't fist them down straight to the striker's feet. And you were at fault with the second goal as well. You were too slow coming out: you put Geoff in a position where he had no option but to clatter Joachim. You'd think you'd never played with Geoff before."

Ted had gone deathly pale. The bad atmosphere returned.

"He sure won't play with him again," someone muttered.

Ted spoke shakily. It cost him a lot. Not many interrupted George Maxton in full flow. "Boss, are you saying that it was my fault Geoff was sent off?"

"It was your fault he had no choice but to take the striker out."

"So it's my fault he was murdered?"

"*I said forget that!*" roared George Maxton.

But Stu was looking keenly at Ted.

Is that what he meant by "They'll blame me for it"? Could Ted have planned to get Geoff sent off?

George continued with his catalogue of errors. Stu thought he'd better concentrate and listen for his own name, which came in due course.

At the very moment Ted was being told to forget it, Inspector Wagstaffe and Sergeant Cumberland were at CID headquarters staring at a letter which had arrived by first-class post that morning. There was no address and no date but the typing was faultless.

Dear Inspector,

There are things you should know which you have not been told.

Ask Rankin why he and Rundle were at loggerheads for many weeks and why, two days

*before Rundle's murder, they had a loud argument
in which Rankin was heard to utter threats of
murder.*

*Ask Ojokwe why he had particular cause to wish
that Rundle was no longer present and why this
cause had rankled for a long time.*

*If you can settle these matters you may be much
closer to an arrest than you are now.*

Yours faithfully,

A well-wisher

Wagstaffe pushed the sheet of paper gloomily
towards Cumberland.

"See what you make of it," he said. "I hate these
anonymous tip-offs."

Cumberland picked the letter up.

"Good quality paper," he said. "Word-processed.
This is done with a laser printer."

"An office network?"

"Could be."

"Like in the office at Radwick Rangers?"

"I'll check."

"I'm not saying this murder has to be an inside
job, but it certainly looks like it."

"Could a player have set the murder up and used
an accomplice to provide himself with the perfect
alibi?" said Cumberland.

"Why not? What about a contract killer? This

24

was a professional job."

"That's big-time stuff for a footballer."

"On their wages they could afford a good one."

"But *how* did they know Rundle would be sent off?"

Wagstaffe didn't answer. He looked at the letter again with acute distaste.

"Check the word-processors in the office at Louring Park," he said. "And get Rankin in first. We'll talk to Ojokwe later. It's the arguments between Rankin and Rundle I'm interested in. We can push him hard on them."

"How so?"

"Look," said Wagstaffe. "I know nothing whatsoever about football, and between you and me I'm rather proud of that fact. But I've found out quite a lot about different sorts of people over the years, and one thing I've noticed is that if two professional sportsmen are having a row, ten-to-one it's either about women or gambling. I don't think this row's about women: that's too easy and besides, I'm sure it would be common knowledge. I reckon it'll be something to do with betting and being cheated. So we'll start off by letting him think we *know* it is, and if we're right he'll just fall into our laps like a plum off a tree."

"And if we're wrong?"

"It won't matter."

*　　*　　*

Annabel was surprised to find her work interrupted by the normally severe Miss Gibson behaving like a fluttery schoolgirl as she introduced Sergeant Cumberland to her.

"I told the sergeant you wouldn't mind letting him see how our word-processing system works," she breathed. "Anything to solve this *terrible* tragedy."

Annabel looked up at the severe face of her boss. Now in her late forties, she must have been an eye-catching figure twenty years ago, Annabel thought. Tall and fair, with blonde hair swept into a bun on her head, she strode through the office like an Amazon.

Annabel dutifully showed Cumberland her work-station, the laser printer and the archive on hard disk of undeleted documents.

"So everything ever printed stays on the archive?" said Sergeant Cumberland.

"Unless the operator deletes it. Or rather . . ." Annabel corrected herself ". . . if Miss Gibson says the operator can delete it."

"And then there's no trace?"

"Gone for ever."

Then Annabel tapped out and printed a few specimen messages for Sergeant Cumberland, who put them in a large envelope, thanked her and departed, leaving her feeling puzzled.

*　　*　　*

No one was really surprised to see a police car and two uniformed policemen outside the training ground. But everybody was shocked when the policemen stepped up to Ted Rankin and asked him to accompany them. As the car left they could see Ted's face looking helplessly out of the rear window.

"He couldn't have," said Nicky Worrall.

"They'll only have a few more routine questions for him," said Ronnie. "I reckon we'll all be in for that."

"But none of us could have done it," insisted Kevin Ray.

Four o'clock in the afternoon. A shaken Ted Rankin was released and allowed home. Inspector Wagstaffe and Sergeant Cumberland looked at each other.

"Well, that was very interesting," said Wagstaffe. "I think we may have got our man."

"Except that we don't know who he paid to do it and we can't get over the fact that nobody could foresee that Rundle would be sent off."

Inspector Wagstaffe looked out of the window at the carpark while Sergeant Cumberland waited patiently. The silence became oppressive.

At length, Wagstaffe spoke.

"Sergeant, you know about football?"

"Oh, yes," said Cumberland. "I used to play. I

could have been a professional. I was picked for the Police against the Army once. And I still watch regularly. I—"

"I don't want an autobiography. Childish past-time for yobs and hooligans, I call it. But no matter. What exactly is a professional foul?"

"It's an offence against the laws of the game committed deliberately and cynically to stop an opponent who would otherwise have scored."

"And that's what Rundle was sent off for?"

"Yes."

"What did he do exactly?"

"The opposing striker was clear and unless he had a sudden brainstorm was bound to score. Ted Rankin in goal was far too slow off his line. Rundle hurtled across and clattered the man off the ball. Clear offence – off he went."

"But if he knew he would be sent off, why do it?"

"He didn't know for sure. A lot of things could have happened. He could have got the ball instead of the man and then everybody would say, 'What a brilliant tackle. You should play for England.' Or the ref could have been lenient and only given him a yellow card. And although there's bound to be a penalty kick awarded, that's not certain to end as a goal. So there's lots of chances to make it worthwhile."

"But the probability is that he'd be sent off."

"Yes."

"You said Rankin was too slow off his line. What exactly does that mean?"

"He should have run out towards the striker to narrow the angle, to make the goal seem smaller, to put himself in the way of the ball. It's amazing how many times what look like certain goals are blocked by a goalkeeper who times his run right and isn't afraid of getting hurt. Ted Rankin's usually good at that."

"But not this time."

"What are you getting at?"

"Would it be possible for Rankin to engineer a situation where Rundle would be bound to get sent off?"

"It's possible . . ."

"So, if he was really quick-witted, he could say to himself, 'I'll stay on my line and give Rundle no option but to commit a professional foul.' "

"I see what you mean. But how did he know that Rundle would go to the dressing-room instead of staying out front and watching?"

"Was Rundle often sent off?"

"Well, yes. He was a bit of a naughty boy on the field, was our Geoff."

"Then find out what he usually did. And if he was in the habit of stalking off the field to change straight away, then we've nearly got our man. Two-thirds of a motive and three quarters of a method."

"But who threw the knife?"

"Don't you worry. I'll break Master Rankin."

4

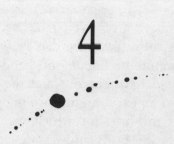

On Tuesday night Rangers were away to West Bromwich Albion. Not a long journey: the coach set off in mid-afternoon and by four o'clock was thrumming along the motorway. Usually the atmosphere was light-hearted: raucous shouts from card-schools and faint tinny thumps from earpieces of Walkmans worn on contented faces with closed eyes would accompany the earnest tactical conversations between Wally and George in their seat at the front.

Today there was an uneasy quiet: no songs, no slap of cards on tables.

"Make them snap out of it," muttered George.

"I can't order them to lighten up," Wally answered.

Ted sat next to Stu. He never said a word the whole journey. His fingers twisted together, his eyes darted nervously round the coach and out of the window.

He shouldn't be playing tonight, thought Stu.

They had brought a reserve goalkeeper, but by the time Ted was substituted the damage was done. In the second minute he flapped his hand weakly at a cross he should have cut out and the West Brom number 8 had an easy tap-in. Five minutes later he dived onto a mis-hit shot which was going wide and the ball hit his body and was deflected into the net. The Hawthorns was a ferment of delight apart from shouts of "What a load of rubbish!" from the Rangers supporters at the Smethwick End.

Ted came off and Chris Kingdon, the reserve, took his place. He trudged to the bench, hesitating before sitting down, as if wondering whether to get changed and then deciding that going into the dressing-room on his own was the last thing he wanted to do. He slumped onto the bench, leaned forward and held his head in his hands.

"Extra training for you tomorrow, my lad," said Wally.

Ted showed no sign of having heard. Nor did he watch Winston Somerset's mighty clearance drop straight to the feet of Dave Prendergast, who in turn slipped it to Stu, who scored his first ever goal for the Rangers.

So it was two-one down at half-time but with everything to play for. "You can do it," George and Wally exhorted the players at half-time.

"I've not seen Ronnie and Kevin work together once yet," said George. "I know they can win any match on their own. Just keep pushing the ball to them and we can hammer this lot."

But Albion refused to be hammered. Wave after wave of Rangers' attacks bore down on the West Brom goal. Ronnie Raikes was inspired: thinking, crafting, teasing the opposition. Kevin had the sort of evening strikers want to forget. He got into all the right positions but he hit post, crossbar, sidenetting. For all his efforts, his luck seemed right out.

So at full-time off they trooped, two games lost in a row. Suddenly the Division 1 championship looked a long way off.

The coach was once again quiet on the dark journey home. George reminded them that after training tomorrow they were to report to Louring Park. Walter Blyton had organized a formal preview of the architect's model of the new North Stand, which would rise over the ruins of the bulldozed North Terrace next season. This raised no spirits.

"Big deal!" an ironic but unidentified voice called from the back of the coach.

George Maxton had no intention of finding out who it was.

Ted sat next to Stu again.

"That was tough, Ted," said Stu.

Ted let out a strange, strangulated groan.

"I'm finished," he answered.

"Never," said Stu. "We all lose a bit of form now and again."

"It's not that. I'm *really* finished."

Stu said nothing but waited.

"Someone's got it in for me. I've been grassed on. And that hound-dog inspector's going to pin Geoff's murder on me. I know it. And he'll make it stick, too."

Stu gasped. "You never—"

"No, of *course* I didn't. But he wants to get someone quick and it's me."

"But how can he do that?"

"He's found out somehow that Geoff and I had a few barneys over the past few weeks. He's clever. I pretty well told him what they were about until I realized he'd trapped me into saying more than I should have. And he's going to say that I paid someone to hide in the dressing-room and kill Geoff when he came in on his own."

"But that's crazy. No one knew Geoff was going to be sent off."

"That's the whole point. They'll put two and

two together, and do you know what they'll find?"

"No?"

"It's true. *I wanted Geoff sent off and I worked it so he was.*"

Stu turned and looked at Ted. In the unreal glow from the motorway lights outside, his face looked pale and haggard. His clenched fist beat on his forehead. This is a man scared out of his wits, thought Stu. Then he remembered the suspicion that had crossed his mind on Monday morning. So he *did* do it.

"Why?" he said.

"Look," said Ted. "I'm going to tell you things that will drive me mad if I don't get them off my chest. But you keep them to yourself."

With a sick feeling inside, Stu realized he might be given a responsibility he wasn't ready for.

"Why me?" he said.

"Because you're new on the squad and I trust you."

"But you hardly know me," said Stu. "Some of the others have been your mates for years."

"Blabbermouths, half of them," said Ted. "They'd shop their grannies for five quid."

"I'm not sure I want to hear this," said Stu.

"Well, you're going to. You've *got* to. Because I'm in the clag right over my head and there's no way out."

Stu felt a swelling of foreboding. He considered

getting up and sitting somewhere else, but he was wedged in by the window. Ted, he thought, was quite capable of forcing him down and keeping him there. This man was desperate. So really it was a sort of duty to listen.

"That Saturday business. I saw the Leicester striker break and I knew he'd score unless I closed him down. And I could have. But I stayed on my line deliberately so Geoff would have to foul him."

"But *why*?"

"I didn't necessarily want Geoff sent off – that was a bonus. What I really wanted was either a goal or a penalty I'd make sure I had no chance with."

"But *why*?" Stu could make no sense out of this.

"To make certain we lost. Two down and I'd be nearly there. Down to ten men and it would be definite."

Stu was baffled. Had Ted gone off his trolley?

"I don't get this," he said.

"Look, I'm telling you because it's all going to come out and I'll be finished anyway, even if I don't get done for murder. I've got more debts than you've had hot dinners. I *need money*, lots of it, fast. And I got in with this betting syndicate and they showed me how to get it."

"How?"

"If you've got a team at the top of the league,

playing like a dream, smashing everyone in sight, you'd get good odds against their losing at home, right?"

"I suppose so."

"Well, that's it. They'd got odds of about ten to one against our getting beaten by Leicester."

"So?"

"They gave me two thousand quid to throw the game. And I said I'd do it if they gave me the money up front to join in the bet. So I'd make twenty grand, no questions asked and no one the wiser."

"You'd never get away with it."

"I would have if Geoff hadn't got himself murdered. Now it's all going to come out and I'll get banned for life at the very least."

"Is that what your rows with Geoff were about?"

"Sort of. He'd got wind of the betting syndicate somehow."

"And he was going to shop you?"

"Not him. He wanted in. But if there were two of us in the know, my cut would be halved and I couldn't afford that. So I warned him off. And he didn't like it."

"What did he do?"

"He threatened to tell Maxton. That's when I yelled at him that I'd kill him. Daftest thing I've ever said. And that's another thing."

"What?"

"We all swore we'd keep quiet when we spoke to the police first off, but *someone* didn't and I'd like to know who it was. That inspector knew all about Geoff and me arguing and he got me into telling him half of it before I realized what was happening."

"But you'll be in the clear, surely. The police will see it was the syndicate who had Geoff murdered."

"Never," said Ted positively. "Murder's not their style. Duffing up, slashing faces, breaking legs maybe – not murder. And definitely not during a game they don't want any attention drawn to. Geoff being murdered is like banner headlines: THIS MATCH WAS BENT."

An uneasy suspicion filled Stu's mind. "What about tonight?"

"Well, what about it?"

"You had to be substituted. We should never have been two down."

"Don't worry. I tried my best tonight, but I couldn't seem to see straight or think right. I'd have taken myself off if Wally hadn't got in first."

He groaned again. "I'm out of my depth, mate," he said. "This isn't *me*. I've had no trouble with the law before. I've not even been nicked for speeding. And now one slip and my whole world's crashing down around me."

Stu looked at Ted's racked and tortured face. A wave of sorrow and sympathy flooded his mind. You were a real idiot to get involved, he thought, but you don't deserve this.

"Try to sleep," he said.

"Fat chance!" replied Ted.

Nevertheless, he put his head back and closed his eyes. A minute later, Stu's ears were filled with the sound of Ted's breathy snores.

As the coach sped down the motorway, Stu thought about what he had heard, and a conviction spread through him that it was knowledge he would rather be without.

Mrs Grundy seemed to have taken a liking to Annabel. The office staff made their own coffee and provided their own biscuits, but often Mrs Grundy would elude Miss Gibson on her way back from the directors in the board room and slip Annabel a couple of éclairs or Bakewell tarts, muttering, "Don't tell anyone, love." And Annabel would thank her, gaze at them wistfully for some time and then give in to temptation. After all, she didn't want to hurt Mrs Grundy's feelings – that slight, sad woman whose history was well known to everyone.

But why was it Annabel Mrs Grundy always went to?

"You're just like the daughter Jim and I always

wanted but never had," Mrs Grundy breathed to her one morning in a moment of rare confidentiality as she passed her a paper plate with two gorgeous-looking Danish pastries on it.

Annabel gave in, sighed and – as she stared at the list of season-ticket holders she was updating – vowed she really would enrol in an aerobics class.

This morning it had been shortbread. As Annabel furtively wiped the crumbs away she wondered how Stu was. She didn't expect to see him till that evening: the players would go straight to the training ground that afternoon, having been given the morning off after last night's match. The extent of that disaster was well known and a matter of concern even in Annabel's office. But she forgot it as she typed away at her lists on a sort of auto-pilot and gave way to daydreaming about Stu – his thick, wavy brown hair, the smile lines on his lean face, his . . .

She came to with a start to find Stu standing in front of her. Far from looking alluring and creased with smile lines, his face was haggard as if after a sleepless night.

"I've got things to tell you," he said. "Ted opened up last night about the killing. I'm worried."

"Not now," she hissed. "Miss Gibson will have a fit. Besides, I've got to finish this lot by twelve."

She worked on, pleased at Stu's urgency but

annoyed that it was bound up with mystery and murder.

Afternoon training had not been happy. The post mortem on the West Brom match had pointed long fingers at Ted, who sat and listened miserably without saying a word in his own defence. His pillorying ended with Wally snapping, "I meant it last night. We'll have an hour together when the rest are gone. I've got you off this preview of the new stand. We'll be concentrating on cutting out crosses. I'll get you your timing back."

The afternoon wore on.

At four o'clock, Inspector Wagstaffe put his phone down for the last time that day and looked at the notes he had made from the conversation.

"Right," he said. "We've got enough to bring Rankin in again. I'll be charging him with murder this evening whether I know who his accomplice is or not, and I'm going to make it stick."

The shadows of trees and the short posts of the practice floodlights lengthened over the training ground. Most of the squad, chastened by the rollocking George Maxton had given them and uninspired by the thought of the new stand, had gone. Only Ted Rankin stayed, wearily listening to Wally's exhortations and picking out of the air the crosses put over by the unfortunate reserves Wally had detailed to stay behind as well.

But at least it kept Ted's mind off his troubles.

"Five o'clock," said Wally. "That's it, lads."

He and the two youngsters put on their tracksuit tops. Wally picked up the footballs they had been using and shoved them into a net bag. They walked away to the clubhouse and changing-rooms.

Ted wanted peace and quiet for a moment, so he didn't move to fish his cap and spare gloves from where he always placed them at the back of the net. He sat down at the foot of the post, put his hands round his knees and closed his eyes as all his troubles raced back into his mind.

"Ted?" said a familiar voice behind him.

He turned round.

The big police Rover braked and stopped in the car-park. Wagstaffe, Cumberland and two uniformed constables entered the clubhouse from the carpark entrance at the very moment Wally and the reserves came through the entrance from the ground.

"Where's Rankin?" demanded Inspector Wagstaffe.

"Following us in," replied Wally, looking round.

"That's funny," said one of the reserves. "He's not there."

"He's sitting at the foot of the goalpost," said the other. "Is he having a kip?"

"I'll soon see," said Wagstaffe grimly.

The four policemen set off across the grass. Wally and the reserves followed a few paces behind. Fifty yards from the goal, all seven started running.

Yes, Ted still sat at the foot of the goal. But his head was held up by the rope round his neck, a rope twisted wickedly and tightly and held in place by a wooden toggle through the loop. His head lolled to one side; his eyes stared and his tongue stuck out.

No, Ted Rankin would never stand trial for murder.

"Garotted!" gasped Wagstaffe. "This is medieval."

5

Stu met Annabel at eight that evening. He had planned to confide in her everything Ted had told him the night before. Part of him said this wouldn't be a good idea: she shouldn't be involved. The other part of him knew she was strong and clear-sighted and wouldn't thank him if he didn't.

But then the news of the second murder broke and it was a shocked, shaking Stu who rang the bell of Annabel's parents' house. She let him in and he slumped into an armchair.

"I know too much," he gabbled. "It'll be me next. These are real sharks behind this betting syndicate and they'll get me to keep me quiet."

"What are you talking about?" said Annabel. "What betting syndicate?"

Stu recounted everything Ted had told him the night before. When he had finished, Annabel spoke.

"So you think these bookies or whoever they are had Geoff killed, then Ted, and now they're after you?"

"Yes," gulped Stu.

"Well, that's stupid. Why would they want to murder you?"

"Because I know too much."

"All you know is what Ted told you. And you said Ted didn't think they had anything to do with Geoff's death."

"How could he know?"

"Because he *knew* them. You don't. He's probably right."

"But now *he's* dead."

"So what? These betting people will want to keep quiet, not go drawing attention to themselves by killing everyone in sight."

"I hope you're right. What shall I do?"

"Tell the police. We'll go together."

Walter Blyton stood by the window in the drawing room of his big house on the hill overlooking the town. A glass of brandy was in his hand. He looked at the lights below him and cursed his luck. Everything had been going so well with the club: his investment was at last beginning to pay off.

Premiership next season, then Europe, with a refurbished ground to match these ambitions – the vistas had seemed endless.

And now this: two murders in five days; press, television and radio swarming round the place for all the wrong reasons; three years' careful work down the chute. It just wasn't true that all publicity was good publicity.

He needed some big announcement, some grand gesture to regain the initiative, to remind the world what sort of club this was – the family club that could reach the heights but could look after its own, like the Jim Grundys of this world.

Jim Grundy. Yes, that was it! The grand gesture formed in his mind. The nation's media would be charmed by his announcement tomorrow at the press conference to unveil the new stand, and all the harmful publicity would be deflected.

He swigged his brandy contentedly. This was why he was rich and others were poor, why he was successful while others failed. Decisive thought and imagination – that's what had got him where he was, and now he was showing these qualities again.

Inspector Wagstaffe was furious. Not only had the murder of his prime suspect showed that his theories were wrong, but the killing must have been no more than five minutes before they found the body. Ted had met his end as Wally and his companions had crossed the pitch and Wagstaffe and his cohorts screeched into the carpark. But no trace of the elusive killer had been found in the gathering darkness, and Wagstaffe had a feeling that none would have been found by next morning either.

"It makes you sick," he said to Cumberland. "With Rundle, all the players were on the field; with Rankin they were all at this blasted preview. Yet someone knew exactly what was going to happen to the very second."

"It doesn't have to have anything to do with any player," said Cumberland. "We know Rankin was involved in some gambling scam and we know there's a link there with Rundle. Uncover the scam and you'll find your killer."

"We'll follow it up," replied Wagstaffe, "but I don't fancy it. These people aren't ones for public executions."

"That's an interesting phrase," said Cumberland.

"What is?"

"Public executions."

"If they were a bit *more* public, we might get somewhere."

The lights in the reception area of the police station were harshly bright. The constable behind the desk recognized Stu, who hadn't quite come to terms yet with the fact that his face was known to total strangers. When Stu said he wanted to make a statement concerning the Radwick Rangers murders, he found himself and Annabel in an interview room with Sergeant Cumberland almost at once. Cumberland sat at the desk, a uniformed constable at his side.

"Sorry the inspector's not here," said Cumberland. "He's gone off duty at last. Has to be up bright and early to interview all you lot again tomorrow morning. But you got in first."

"I've got information," said Stu.

"I'm glad someone has. Sit down and I'll get the tape-recorder ready."

Stu recorded the whole of his conversation with Ted and then Sergeant Cumberland spoke the time and date into the microphone and stopped the machine. He removed the cassette and the constable took it away.

"I'll have that typed up. You can read it over and sign it."

"Is that all?" said Stu.

"Just one or two things off the record. Ted Rankin was right. We were going to charge him because we'd got everything right, even down to his meaning to get Rundle sent off. It fitted. We just needed to break him down into telling us who his hired contract man was. Now he's dead and the whole thing's blown sky-high. What clinched it for us was getting over the problem of *knowing* that Rundle would be in the dressing-room. Now Rankin's dead, that's a bigger mystery than ever."

"But if the killer's in this betting syndicate, don't I need police protection or something?"

"Look, lad, we're following up that lead. If they're who we think they are, then they'll want to keep quiet. Rundle and Rankin are both gone, so they won't talk any more. You don't even know who these people are and you certainly haven't had any money off them, so they couldn't care less about you. You're not a grass: you just helped us with our inquiries."

"Can I go, then?" said Stu.

"In a minute," said Cumberland. "Now you're here I may as well ask you what we'll be asking all the players tomorrow. What were your movements between training and five o'clock today when Rankin's body was found?"

Stu answered at once. "I was showered and changed at 4.15," he said. "Then I went back to Louring Park because Mr Blyton wanted us all there to see the model of the new North Stand. He's going to announce it at the press conference this morning."

"That's not the only thing he'll be announcing," said Cumberland grimly.

"We were all there," said Stu.

"The whole squad?"

"I think so. I can't think of any who weren't – except Wally and Ted and the two lads he kept back."

Sergeant Cumberland drummed his fingers distractedly on the desk. The constable came back in with typed sheets of paper. Stu read them through, agreed they were a fair account of what he had said, and signed. Cumberland stood up.

"OK," he said. "That's it. Thanks for coming – I appreciate it."

Annabel and Stu left. Outside, they both thought of the same question which even now was making Sergeant Cumberland pound his head with his fists as he sat alone in the interview room.

How did this elusive killer know so exactly the victims' movements when they didn't know them themselves?

Walter Blyton's press conference was delayed for two hours while the police finished their routine questioning of everyone who had been at the training ground and Louring Park the previous afternoon. What Stu had said was echoed by everyone else. Once again, every suspect had a cast-iron alibi.

Walter Blyton had hoped for an audience consisting of football journalists and perhaps a few architectural correspondents from the posh papers. Not surprisingly, however, the stadium was crowded with reporters from every paper as well as TV and radio. The conference – and the model of the futuristic new stand – had to be transferred from the boardroom to the indoor gym.

Stu, no longer needed by the police, slipped in to watch. The portly Blyton in his blue suit looked out of place amid the weight-training machines and other apparatus. A trestle table stood at the front covered with green baize cloth and the model of the stand was covered with a white drape. Behind the table sat Walter Blyton, John Forbes, George Maxton and several directors – and, Stu was puzzled to see, Mrs Grundy. Blyton's great idea was meant as a surprise. Still in her brown tea-lady's uniform, Mrs Grundy sat next to Blyton, her eyes cast down, looking supremely embarrassed. Stu also noticed that Inspector Wagstaffe had slipped into the gym and was standing unobtrusively but watchfully at the back.

The noise was tremendous. Reporters shouted questions which nobody had a chance of hearing, let alone answering. None were about the new stand: all were about the murders.

Blyton raised his hand for silence. No use whatsoever. George Maxton stood up, impressive and forbidding. He picked up the microphone.

"Belt up!" he roared.

The noise subsided. George sat and Blyton spoke.

"This great club is living through dark days," he said. "But there is always light at the end of the tunnel and we must look to better times ahead when football is once again our only concern and we retake our rightful place in the Premiership as one of the great powers in the land."

"Hear, hear!" said the directors in unison.

"Get on with it!" shouted a voice from the back.

"If you will let me," said Blyton. "As you know, Louring Park, like all other major grounds, is to become an all-seater stadium. This means hard decisions for us. The North Terrace – like Liverpool's Kop, Villa's Holte End, Arsenal's North Bank – has deep and sentimental connections for our club. Such traditions are not easily cast aside, but the decision is made. That famous bank of terracing must go, to be replaced by – this."

Blyton whisked the veil away, exposing the silver cantilever structure. With its dramatic roof sweeping over the executive boxes seemingly suspended in mid-air and its cherry-red seats with RANGERS picked out in yellow, it looked as if an aircraft hangar, a suspension bridge, a *Toys 'Я' Us* superstore and a theatre had been jumbled up together.

There was silence in the gym.

"Not bad," someone said eventually.

"Not as good as Newcastle's," said someone else.

If Walter Blyton had hoped for ecstasy, he was disappointed. But he stuck to his guns.

"I said we must look at our traditions," he said. "And we must salute the qualities that have made this club great. I have deliberated much on what to call the new stand, and I believe I have the answer. Let me introduce to you someone who typifies the family spirit and the civic pride of Radwick Rangers. Stand up, Mrs Grundy."

The small figure, her wispy auburn hair showing under the white cap, rose diffidently.

"Some of you know her story," said Blyton. "For those who do not, her husband Jim was for forty years a regular on the North Terrace. He lived for this club. When he died his ashes were spread over the pitch. He *is* our club: his widow is our club. For that reason I have the greatest pleasure in announcing that this wonderful new structure is to be known as the Jim Grundy Memorial Stand."

The directors behind the table clapped vigorously. From the ranks of reporters there was silence. Mrs Grundy gazed with submissive admiration at Blyton. Stu looked round at the scene. Cameras were pointed at the tea-lady and flashes went off. The media were waking up to a possible story. Stu waited for the questions to start.

"Mrs Grundy, how do you feel about your late husband's name being used in this way?"

There was an inaudible mutter from the down-cast face. Howls of discontent came from the assembled gentlefolk of the press. Walter Blyton shoved the microphone into Mrs Grundy's hands.

"I'm very proud and I'm sure my Jim would have been likewise."

"Mrs Grundy, are you happy for your husband's name to be associated with a cheap publicity stunt?"

"Well, I . . ."

"Mrs Grundy, do you think it's right that this club should exploit you just to divert attention from the fact that there's a serial killer stalking the place?"

"I don't—"

"Mrs Grundy—"

Walter Blyton rose to his feet in protest. Before he could speak, George Maxton was by his side and roaring.

"Quiet! You bullies, you've no right to hound someone who can't defend herself!"

Then he sat down again, his face red and twitching with anger. For a moment it looked to Stu as if the whole conference would break up in disorder, then a woman stood up.

"Mrs Grundy!" her clear voice called.

The noise died.

"Mrs Grundy, my readers will be very interested in your late husband and you. I'm wondering if there are any photographs we can see – something to recreate for our readers the life of so steadfast and faithful a man."

"Oh, yes," said Mrs Grundy. "I've got a lot of old photographs of Jim. You can see them if you want."

Blyton stood up.

"This collection of photographs Mrs Grundy has mentioned will be put into an album which will be placed in my possession. Copies can be made and all fees will go to Mrs Grundy. But you must approach me for permission."

He sat down again.

Interest in Mrs Grundy seemed to evaporate as quickly as it had come. A reporter at the front stood up and looked straight at Blyton.

"Now you've played your little diversionary tactic, are you going to tell us anything about these murders?"

"I can't say anything you don't already know. You'll have to ask the police—"

"Fat lot they'll tell us," came a roar from the back.

Stu thought he'd seen enough. He slipped out of the gym and left them to it.

6

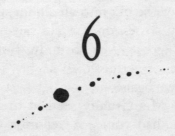

Thursday afternoon: training again. Friday would see the long journey to Sunderland, with a night spent in a hotel in Durham. Meanwhile, the players who gathered for five-a-side games and practising dead ball situations were quiet. A pall of fear and depression had settled over the ground. The far goal where Ted had met his end was shunned.

The session started badly.

"Regular first-team goalie are we now?" Nicky Worrall had said to Chris Kingdon. "Talent always wins at this club."

It took Winston Somerset and Dave Prendergast between them to restrain Chris from setting about him.

"You bad-mouthed little toerag!" shouted Chris.

As usual, Ronnie calmed them all down.

"This isn't what we're here for," he said. "We've got a hard game on Saturday, so concentrate on it."

Everybody on the field, though, was half-hearted. George and Wally ran around exhorting players to greater efforts – to no avail. Afterwards, when they were all together waiting for manager and coach to give a run-down on the Sunderland team and talk about tactics, George entered and barked at them furiously.

"You're supposed to be professionals. You're supposed to be highly-trained, single-minded athletes. And what do I find? You're a miserable bunch of snivelling kids afraid of their own shadows."

Kevin interrupted – a daring thing to do. Heads turned to him in admiration.

"It's all right for you, boss," he said. "But it's us this killer's after. Picking off players one by one – who's next? It could be any one of us."

There was a rumble of agreement. Stu realized that Kevin had spoken exactly what was in everyone's mind but what they were all afraid to say out loud.

George's voice softened.

"All right," he said. "I know how you must feel. But don't worry – the police have got this well in hand. They know why Geoff and Ted were killed. It's to do with betting and match-fixing."

"So they say," muttered someone.

"So unless any others of you are involved, there's nothing to fear. And if any of you are . . ." and here his voice became menacing again ". . . you'll have me to watch out for, not some deranged serial killer. Because I won't have you at this club. I'll have you out of the game for life. Now, let's think about Saturday."

The discussion went on for an hour. At five, George and Wally left the room.

There was no move to follow them. Some instinct kept the players back, like the beleaguered, besieged garrison of a little fort.

"Do you think he's right about this match-fixing thing?" said Lee Boatman.

"We're off the hook if he is," said Winston.

"Does it often happen?" said Ossie.

Ronnie spoke. "More than you'd think," he said. "And when it's found out, there's all hell to pay."

"How so?" said Winston.

"Well, there was the big scandal back in the sixties with some Sheffield Wednesday players. They were banned for life. And there were criminal charges: they came up for trial and got prison as well. And there were more cases which didn't get as far. I remember a newspaper report saying it happened at a club down south – though it only came out years later. Their goalkeeper threw a home game when they were just on the point of winning the old Third Division. He let in three goals and no one suspected. In fact, he looked so good that the opponents made an offer for him. But that Sheffield Wednesday scandal was bad. It rocked the game. So did the one at City when I was there – the Billy Manners affair."

"Tell us about it," said Kevin.

"But I've already told you," said Ronnie. "A fortnight ago, on the coach to Southend."

"Well, tell the rest, then. It's a tale worth hearing."

The players all grouped round Ronnie as he started.

"This happened in the early seventies. I was only sixteen and I was an apprentice at City. But I was marked out as a player to watch and I often trained with the first team. The season after, when I was seventeen, I was the youngest player ever in City's first team. Like you now, Stu."

Stu smiled. "If I thought I'd have a career a quarter as good as yours I'd be over the moon," he said.

"Well, I didn't know what was going to happen then any more than you do now," said Ronnie. "Anyway, that's where I first met George Maxton. He was a central defender: he was a *rock*. And he helped me a lot – looked after me, advised me, kept me out of trouble. When you're the age I was, you think you're bound to go all the way –

win the League, the cup, play in Europe, play for England, take part in *A Question of Sport*. You usually have to settle for a lot less. But even then George could see that if I was looked after, I could go far. He showed me then what a good manager he'd make. He kept in touch long after we'd gone our separate ways. But he remembered me when he needed me and when I needed him. That's why I'm here."

"What's this got to do with match-fixing?" said Ossie Canklow.

"Be patient," said Ronnie. "That City team was brilliant: two League Championships, the FA Cup, the European Cup-Winners Cup once – all in four years. It had everything: George at the centre of things, calm, strong, never making a mistake. And he was a regular for Scotland as well. Freddy Cash and Alan Askey were deadly strikers. But the brains at the heart of it all – that was Billy Manners."

"Everyone's heard of him," said Lee Boatman. "Where is he now?"

"Where indeed?" said Ronnie. "I've no idea. Even if he's still alive. But he was magic, was Billy Manners. The most thinking, skilful player I've ever seen. He could read a game like a book; he could pace himself, time everything perfectly, slow the game right down to suit himself. He *always* seemed to have space, no matter how hard the tackles were going in. He made that City team."

"So how did he get involved in throwing matches?" said Winston.

"God knows," said Ronnie. "He lived for City. He was a real one-club man, like Pompey's Jimmy Dickinson. Just not interested in going anywhere else. When it all came out, the shock nearly ruined the club. He had money worries and a wife who wanted a bit more than he could give her. He got in with some pretty high-powered gamblers, had a sure-fire proposition put to him, couldn't resist it. After all, who cares if you lose to a team that's already relegated and when you're eight points clear at the top? And Billy could do it without anyone ever suspecting. He could put a thirty-yard pass straight to the foot of an opponent and everyone would blame the City player it seemed meant for. 'Billy thinking too quickly for the rest of us again,' is what we'd all say. He once gave three goals away like that against Burnley. It's on video: I've got a copy. Now you know what's happening, you can see how he does it. But nobody could ever have suspected at the time."

"So how was he found out?" Stu asked.

"Someone grassed on him. Anonymous tip-off, big investigation, Billy found guilty, banned for life. He was lucky he didn't go for trial and get gaol like the ones before him. Even without that, it broke him."

"What did he do afterwards?" asked Ossie.

"I don't know. I heard he left his wife and kid. It was as if he wanted the world to swallow him up – go where he'd not be recognized, change his name perhaps and live alone with his shame."

"Surely someone looked for him?" said Stu. "What about newspapers?"

"You know the press," said Ronnie. "The next big story comes along: the old one's forgotten. Billy didn't disappear overnight. He wasn't Lord Lucan. It was just that one day nobody knew where he was. You know what they say, 'I wonder what became of so-and-so?' Nobody knows so everyone forgets."

The players were silent. Then Ade spoke.

"That's bad," he said. "You can't live without your self-respect. But if I were him I'd have fought back."

"Things like that take people different ways," said Ronnie. "At least in Billy's case there were no murders involved – just a long decline for City so they're only now scrambling back into the Premiership along with us."

"Anyway," said Dave Prendergast, "the manager's right. If Ted and Geoff were killed because of a match-fixing row then we *are* all off the hook. Unless someone else is involved."

He looked round and saw the lack of conviction in all the faces which stared back at him.

"I bet you wish you'd never come here," said Kevin.

The conversation seemed over. Ronnie's story about the past had depressed them even more. They all got up to leave.

"I don't think our trouble has got anything to do with throwing games," said Winston. "I think we're all still in danger. I feel it in my bones."

"Thanks, Winston," said Nicky. "That's just what we wanted to hear."

Annabel was full of the morning's events. She and Stu sat in the sitting room of her parents' house. They had gone away for a couple of days.

"You should have seen Mrs Grundy after that press conference," she said. "She really came alive for the first time since I've known her. She came into the office *loaded* with cakes and a couple of bottles of wine—"

"Nicked from the boardroom, no doubt," said Stu.

"Not nicked," said Annabel. "They let her take things. Mr Blyton thinks she's some sort of mascot, especially after this morning. And if Miss Gibson thought there was any funny business she wouldn't have let her in."

"That Gibson woman's a menace," said Stu. "She's like the figurehead on a clipper ship. Twenty years ago I bet she was really something."

"I dare you to tell her that," said Annabel.

"Not me," said Stu. "Anyway, it doesn't alter the

fact that Blyton only used Mrs Grundy and her old man to get the media off his back over the murders."

"Don't be so cynical," said Annabel. "It was a lovely thing to do. It's certainly made a new woman of Mrs Grundy. 'My Jim would be so proud,' she kept on saying. 'Fancy, a whole new stand named after him.' It's really made her come out of her shell."

"Well, it's all right for some," said Stu, "but it doesn't help us one bit."

Annabel snuggled up to Stu and put her head on his shoulder.

"Poor Stu," she said. "I know it's horrible having all this hanging over you. But at least something's made Mrs Grundy happy."

"Never mind Mrs Grundy," said Stu, pulling her closer. "I know what would make me happy." He began to stroke her hair, and she turned her face towards his.

Stu was very happy as he stepped onto the coach. Annabel was the best thing – along with his contract with Rangers – that had ever happened to him. He leaned back in his seat, his brain teeming with thoughts of her, unaware of the deep and fearful depression surrounding him.

Everyone was on board and the kit was all stowed away. The coach set off.

George and Wally stood at the front and surveyed

the squad. There were no card-schools, no raucous jokes: just a solid, sullen silence.

"Look at them," said George. "Scared witless. They're in no shape to play tomorrow."

"Except young Stu. Look at *him*. Eyes closed, daft grin on his face – what's he been up to?"

"Never mind him," said George. "The rest look like they're on the tumbril, not the team coach. And there's a long journey ahead of us. They'll be suicidal by the end of it."

"They're like little children, for all they're so big and macho," said Wally. "Little children who need comforting. They're past being yelled at."

"Wally, you're right. And what's the best way of comforting children?"

"You tell me."

"Tell them a story."

George whispered to the driver, who handed him the public address microphone. "And that, Wally, is what I'm going to do."

Inspector Wagstaffe and Sergeant Cumberland were back to square one. As the Rangers' coach sped northwards, they sat in Wagstaffe's office and looked helplessly at each other. Wagstaffe took the anonymous letter which had put him on to Ted Rankin and smoothed it out on the desk.

"Our only positive lead," he said, "and look where it's got us."

"It wasn't only about Rankin," said Cumberland. They looked again at the end of the letter.

Ask Ojokwe why he had particular cause to wish that Rundle was no longer present and why this cause had rankled for a long time.

If you can settle these matters you may be much closer to an arrest than you are now.

"And maybe not," said Cumberland.

"What do we know about Ade Ojokwe?" said Cumberland.

"Comes from Nigeria. Born in Lagos. Spotted by Wally Kerns two years ago when he took an England Youth Team on tour. Been at Radwick now for over a year. Lovely little player: fast and clever. The fans love him."

"But Rundle didn't. Why not, I wonder? Racial abuse, perhaps? From what we've heard about Rundle, he wasn't the most sensitive soul. He might not be too fussy about what he said to people."

"Remember this, though," said Cumberland. "If you want a good example of ethnic integration in this day and age you don't need to look further than the playing staff of a professional football club. Everything else gets forgotten when there's mutual respect based on ability and co-operation."

"That sounds a rosy-tinted view to me," said Wagstaffe.

"It's true," said Cumberland.

"So we're saying everyone might have been sweetness and light at Radwick except Rundle?"

"It looks like it."

"But Ojokwe's not the only black player in the first team squad. What about Winston Somerset? Why didn't the letter mention him?"

Cumberland thought for a moment. Then: "Because Winston's big and Ade's little."

"So Rundle would only needle Ojokwe?"

"It looks like it."

"So why didn't Somerset protect him?"

"I don't suppose Rundle was too blatant about his abuse. And anyway, Ade's from Nigeria and Winston's from Jamaica. They're no more likely to stick together than a Frenchman is with a Swede."

"Hmm," said Wagstaffe doubtfully. Then: "On Monday we get Ojokwe in here. Right?"

7

George Maxton stood at the front of the coach and looked at the seats facing him. He saw strained, morose faces staring back. The driver had switched off the incessant background music. George touched the microphone to check it was working, then he started talking. His lulling voice with its hypnotic Scots burr filled all ears. He was an indulgent, kind father telling bedtime stories to calm his frightened children into soft sleep.

"I've told you before and I'll tell you again. Every one of you is here because I put you here. I think you're good – and if I think you're good then you *are* good. And if you're real players, real professionals, you play to a certain standard no matter what's on your mind. *Nothing* gets in the way: not sorrow, not loss, not fear of injury, not fear of death. *Nothing.*"

He paused. The faces hadn't changed, but they were listening intently.

"Some of you are just starting, some are nearly finished. Some will go out of the game for ever, some will be managers like me. And you'll all have troubles, probably bigger than you're having now. And you mustn't let them get you down. Look at me, for example. I'm going to tell you a tale now about something I'll never forget and it will show you you're not the only ones that football has put through hell."

The coach was leaving the suburbs of Radwick. Neat houses on either side of the dual-carriageway were giving way to open countryside.

"I was born in a mining village near Glasgow. Football was the great religion there, and almost the only way out of the place. So I was football daft as soon as I could walk. I played league football early: Motherwell, St Mirren – decent Scottish clubs both of them, and I would have been content to stay there because I was happy.

"But then along came a scout from an English club and spotted me. And soon I was meeting the person who's been the most important to me in my whole life – more than parents, wife, children. Think of that: if you're in football, that's how it's got to be."

Ronnie, as always, sat next to Kevin. He nudged him.

"Bet you I know who he means."

"Luke Jackson, then manager of City," said George.

"Told you," muttered Ronnie.

"Luke was the greatest manager of the greatest team since the war. He was like a father to me, to us all. Now, lads, I know you get brassed off with me a lot of the time. You'd not be human if you didn't. But remember: it's Luke Jackson I model myself on and when I fail it's my fault, not his."

"I never thought I'd hear George the Confessor," whispered Kevin. "Things must be pretty bad."

The coach had reached the motorway junction and was heading down the slip road.

"Anyway," continued George, "City were the best team of the sixties and seventies – no doubt of it. And I was part of it. Once you're in the Premiership, you could be as good. I mean it."

They were now bowling along at a steady seventy in the middle lane. The manager had everyone's full, rapt attention.

"That team was full of great players. Luke Jackson was the first to see what they could be and made them his way. Frankie Saunders in goal: Welsh international. Like a leaping gazelle – I've never seen anything like him. Freddy Cash and Alan Askey – the deadly duo: the sort of partnership I see Ronnie and Kevin developing into. But the greatest of all, the one who turned a good team into a great one, was Billy Manners."

Stu had been listening of course but, unlike the others, with only part of his attention. Most of his thoughts were taken up with last night and Annabel; also, he was disturbed at being alone in his seat when last time he had sat next to Ted. But the name Billy Manners made him sit up suddenly. That name had surfaced from nowhere twice in three days. He now listened keenly.

"Billy was the greatest. You can talk about Ossie Ardiles, Gazza, Cruyff, Beckenbauer, Glenn Hoddle. But not even Paddy Crerand was as thoughtful and creative as Billy. And none of them, I don't care what anyone says, had his skill. And, do you know, he didn't cost a penny. He was found playing on a local park. But Luke Jackson took one look and he *knew*. Money couldn't buy a player like Billy Manners nowadays. Playing alongside him was the greatest privilege of my life."

"Big talk," whispered Kevin.

"He's right," replied Ronnie. "You never saw him."

"My four years with City were the best of my life," said George. "I know I had good times afterwards at Chelsea and Arsenal, Newcastle and Southampton. But those years were special and magic."

71

A Jaguar sped past in the outer lane at over a hundred miles an hour. A police car hurtled after it.

"But they ended. Nothing perfect can last. Perfection can't get better: it has to decline. That's the way of the world. Corruption sets in . . ." Stu noticed a sort of venom in the manager's voice as he spoke the word *corruption* ". . . and the worm eats away at the rose."

The police car and the Jaguar had stopped on the hard shoulder. As the coach passed, the players could see a policeman getting out and marching towards the Jaguar. Then they dwindled away to play out their own little drama.

"The times I remember!" said George. "The day we beat Manchester United five-nil at Old Trafford and Billy Manners gave the greatest performance I've ever seen from one player. The way he turned the Leeds defence to send Alan Askey away to score the winner in the 1970 Cup Final. How he beat Liverpool on his own in the match which gave us the points to win the League in 1971. And how he played Bayern Munich off the park at the San Siro the night we won the European Cup-Winners Cup.

"And it all ended. When the world's at your feet, you throw it all away. And that's what Billy did. Because behind all that talent was greed. He was hungry for money. He was well paid at City:

they wouldn't see him short. Foreign clubs wanted him: he wouldn't go. Greedy and scared at the same time. Perhaps he should have gone."

George paused. Every face in the coach was looking at him enthralled. He knew he had his audience hooked.

"You've only got to look at Olympique Marseille to see what happens when you think you're on top and no one can touch you. You *can't* do wrong: you're unassailable, beyond the laws of ordinary mortals. So temptation came Billy's way. And what did he do? He threw games for money – games which didn't matter to the club. But it wasn't right. And I could see what he was doing. You don't play alongside someone week after week, season after season, and not know what he's up to. I *noticed* when the cross-field ball was carefully misplaced to be intercepted, when he'd roll the back pass just a few inches out of true so it reached their forward and not our goalkeeper. Everyone blamed our lads for not being quite on his wavelength, but I knew better.

"I used to lie awake all night worrying about it. What should I do? Should I tell anyone? Billy was my best friend: we roomed together on away games. It got so I couldn't speak to him. My own game suffered. It was my worst time. And I've never told anyone before today that I *knew* what was going on."

Ronnie whispered again to Kevin, who was staring transfixed at George Maxton.

"This is amazing!" he said.

"And then it all came out," said George. "Someone found out: perhaps a bookie spoke out, perhaps Billy upset one of the men who was using him. Anyway, suddenly there were headlines in *The Sun* and *News of the World*, and inside two days everyone was at it. There was a Football Association inquiry and I testified at it. I told them I never had the slightest inkling about what was going on, because I wanted to be loyal to my friend and because there was no way I could prove my suspicions. But what I could say was that though we roomed together, he'd never given the slightest hint there was anything wrong.

"Well, he was found guilty and banned from all contact with the game for life. He nearly faced trial and prison. He was lucky there were no criminal charges brought; others who'd done what he did got time for it. Even so, that was the worst shock I ever had. The team broke up: we all wanted to go. I went to Chelsea and watched from afar. City had already won the League that season: next season they were relegated – a ruined club. They even went down to the Fourth Division for a couple of seasons. It's taken them over twenty years to get back to anything like what they were, and if they go up to the Premiership with us this season, I'll be as happy for them as I will be for us."

"He means that," said Ronnie. "So will I."

"And Billy? Someone told me he'd changed his name and gone abroad. If he did, I'd bet a month's wages he's coaching teams in Africa or the Far East where the game's really taking off. Because I can't see him staying alive without football."

"Neither can I," muttered Ronnie. "I'd love to believe that."

"Why shouldn't he be?" said Kevin.

"Well, George, you old devil," Ronnie said, as if to himself. "I've known you all these years and you've always been fair but you've always been distant as well. Nobody's got close to you, nobody's known what you're really thinking. And you choose this moment to bare your soul to us in public."

"I think he knows exactly what he's doing," said Kevin.

"You don't have to tell me that," said Ronnie.

George was continuing.

"So there you are. This tragedy of Geoff and Ted and the reasons behind it brought back the memory of Billy Manners and my own dark time. Nobody died then, but feelings ran high when it all came out, and perhaps somebody could have. And perhaps we could say that the deaths of Geoff and Ted have nipped that kind of trouble in the bud for us. Because it's over now. There's no more canker at Radwick. I know it. I know how you feel: I know it will pass. I've told you things I've never told anyone before to show you I'm right. So think on. You're professionals. You're good. You'll rise above this. I'm with you. Remember that."

He sat down. For a moment there was no sound at all except the steady roar of the coach's diesel engine as it swept north onto the A1. Then first Winston, then Dave, then Lee, then Chris, then Ade, then Stu, then Ronnie and Kevin, then Nicky, then everybody else stood up. Tentative at first, then stronger, the clapping started. The standing ovation lasted two full minutes. When it died away, the players sat down again. Faces were relaxed, conversations animated. By Wetherby, the first card-school had started.

"I was right," said Cumberland. "I've had a few words with players in the reserve squad. Ade and Winston aren't particular friends. They don't even room together on away games. Winston rooms with Chris Kingdon usually, Ade with Lee Boatman. And they say there's no doubt that Ade wasn't happy when Rundle was around. Since the murder they're quite convinced that once the shock was over Ade has tried hard to seem as upset as everybody else, but he can't conceal the fact that he's mighty relieved."

"Well, it's something," said Wagstaffe. "As slim

a lead as I've ever followed, but our anonymous letter-writer seems to know more than anyone else does."

"If we knew who wrote the letter we'd be a lot better off," said Cumberland. "High-tech laser printers beat letters cut out of newspaper headlines any day for keeping your identity secret."

"We'll have a word with Master Ojokwe first thing Monday, just to eliminate him." Wagstaffe stared gloomily through the window. "We've got to talk to *somebody*. We're getting nowhere."

A lovely day at Roker Park. Rangers were in their all-blue away strip when they ran out onto the pitch and saluted the three thousand chanting supporters massed at the uncovered Roker End, who had faithfully made the long journey from Radwick. Then out came Sunderland in their famous red and white stripes and the packed ground waited.

Rangers were back at their best. They played as if weights had fallen from their shoulders and shackles from their legs. Kevin and Ronnie were working well. Kevin got himself into two good positions through his perceptive understanding with Ronnie. He hit a post from eight yards and put the ball just wide from ten. But everyone felt goals would come. A confidence spread that had been lacking at West Brom. When Sunderland took the lead it was nobody's fault – simply a good move and a shot no goalkeeper could have stopped. This time, no Rangers head went down, no inevitability of defeat suffused the team. And the player who did the most was Ade Ojokwe. He seemed inspired. Five minutes into the second half he had his reward. He picked up the ball outside the Radwick penalty area, pushed out a perfect pass to Stu, collected Stu's return and was off on a mazy run, leaving five Sunderland players gasping in his wake. As the goalkeeper rushed out, he calmly lobbed the ball over his head from twenty yards.

George and Wally leapt up in the dugout and punched the air.

"That *has* to be the best individual goal I've ever seen!" yelled Wally.

Ade, his arms spread wide, rushed towards the ecstatic Rangers fans. The rest of the team followed. The tune of "Guantanamera" emerged out of the cheering:

One Ade Ojokwe,
There's only one Ade Ojokwe,
One Ade O-jo-kwe,
There's only one Ade O-jo-kwe.

The tune dipped low with its last two long notes and was lost in renewed cheers. Ade and the rest loped back to restart the game.

And Rangers nearly won it, too. Three minutes from the end a blistering shot from Kevin hit a post: his blast from the rebound was deflected over the bar. He rose high to head the resulting corner downwards and shaved the post by a couple of inches with the goalkeeper beaten.

He stood still, head in his hands. Ronnie ran up and put an arm round his shoulders.

"*Unlucky*, Kevin!" he said.

"What's the matter with me?" said Kevin. "I should be having these chances for breakfast."

"Everybody has these spells," said Ronnie as they ran upfield to face the goalkick.

But at the end, George Maxton clapped his team off the field and spoke to them warmly in the dressing-room.

"A draw at Roker's a good result in anyone's book," he said. "I'm proud of you. You've done well."

The dressing-room atmosphere wasn't boisterous, as it often was after a good away result. Rather it was reflective, relieved. The players believed in themselves again.

They filed back on the coach happy to hear City had drawn as well. Rangers were still top, though only just. Before the coach left, Wally gave them a reminder.

"Photocall at the ground Monday afternoon. Everyone to be there. Some football magazine. Next month, you'll be a poster pinned to the walls of the nation's bedrooms."

"Can't wait," said Kevin.

The coach left. Now the card-schools started at once and didn't stop until the coach turned off the A1 and stopped outside the restaurant where the team dinner had been booked.

Inside the restaurant, Stu found himself sitting next to Ronnie. Kevin had wandered off with Ossie. Stu was still slightly in awe of his captain, this man who had savoured pretty well every experience the game of football had to offer. So, after the usual exchange of "You were great today" and "So were you", he subsided into silence. Ronnie looked distracted, but halfway through his steak and chips, he spoke.

"What did you make of what the boss told us on the way up?"

"It was fascinating," said Stu. "I just thought it was strange that Billy Manners got mentioned twice in three days."

"Yeah. Funny coincidence," said Ronnie. "After this rotten business about Geoff and Ted the two of us were bound to be thinking along the same lines. But there's something that worries me."

"What's that?"

"The way the boss told it. That's not how I remember it happening."

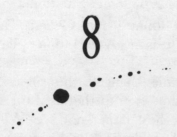

8

When they returned to the coach, Stu sat alone in the seat he used to share with Ted and started thinking about what Ronnie had told him. It was odd.

"The boss said he didn't know how the scandal came out: perhaps some punter in the know who felt cheated went to the papers and the first anyone knew of it was headlines in *The Sun*. Well, that's not how it was. Everybody knew what had happened, even me, the newest apprentice. Someone grassed on him. Someone who knew exactly what Billy had done wrote anonymously to the chairman and he told the Football Association. He had no option. It was all known at the club *before* the papers got hold of it."

"So?" said Stu. "What's the problem? He's probably forgotten."

"You don't forget things like that," said Ronnie. "Not when they're so close to you."

"Perhaps he thought the way he told it would make a better story."

"No," said Ronnie. "Not George. There must be some other reason. And I don't like what I'm thinking."

Then Ronnie changed the subject. His half-closed eyes shut even further as if there was something outside he'd rather not see. When Stu was leaning comfortably back in his coach seat he fell to wondering what it was.

Surely it couldn't be that George Maxton had falsified a true story because it was *he* who had grassed on Billy Manners?

Impossible. They were obviously close and re-spected each other for being at the top of their craft. Nobody who spoke of another person in the terms George Maxton had used of Billy Manners could grass on him. Except – what had George said? "Greedy and scared at the same time." That wasn't too friendly.

But it sounded true. And real friends take you warts and all, so this was no reason to think George split on his great mate. No, Ronnie had got it wrong. After all, he hadn't been close to the centre of things then – he was just a sixteen-year-old apprentice.

So why was he so certain?

Anyway, did it matter?

Well, it did if Ronnie was beginning to have doubts about the man who'd taken him off the scrapheap and rescued his career. That would be a terrible blow to him.

Especially after George Maxton, that strong Scot who minced no words, had brought himself to do something out of character which must have cost him a lot – had confided things about himself to his team purely to remotivate them. That must have gone against the grain. Yet to Stu, it made him seem a warmer person who was even worthier of respect than the distant, unsmiling guru who had ruled his life at the club until now.

So why place a deliberate lie at the heart of the story?

The questions wound round and round inside his brain as the coach neared Radwick. His eyes closed and as he dozed, Billy Manners became mixed up with Ted Rankin and Geoff Rundle. When he finally slept, there was the first, merest flicker of understanding in his mind.

Stu spent Sunday with Annabel. They drove out into the country, had lunch at a country club the players often used, then headed up into the hills. They drove to where it was high and the cold air was clear and swept the mind free of cobwebs.

They stopped and got out.

Stu couldn't let the questionings of the night before rest.

"Why should George change the story? Was *he* the anonymous tip-off? And why have I got this idea in my head that it's all connected with what's happening now?"

"Spilling the beans on his friend, whatever he's done, doesn't sound like the George Maxton we see in the office," said Annabel. "If there's anyone you could call 'straight as a die', it's him. But confessing to you lot like that doesn't sound like him either. There's more to your boss than meets the eye."

"But how can the two stories be connected?"

"I don't know. Let's see."

"How?"

"By looking," said Annabel patiently, "at what they've got in common."

"All right," said Stu. "Well, first, they both concern match-fixing. Players deliberately making their teams lose so they can clean up on bets."

"Second," said Annabel, "George Maxton was involved in both, as player in the first and manager in the second."

"And third," said Stu, "so was Ronnie Raikes. A player at both clubs when the match-fixing happened."

"And fourth?" said Annabel.

"God knows," said Stu.

"Ronnie wouldn't be involved in anything like that, would he?" said Annabel.

"Surely not. They're at each end of his career. The first time he had everything still to gain, now he's got too much to lose."

Stu spoke positively, but he couldn't help a doubt forming in his mind.

"I like Ronnie," said Annabel. "He's dreamy."

"What's this?" said Stu. "The attractions of the older man?"

"Don't worry," said Annabel.

"What about George?"

"Oh, I wouldn't fancy him," said Annabel.

"That's not what I meant. Would he be involved in match-fixing?"

"You know him better than I do.'"

"I'm beginning to wonder. But I'm sure he wouldn't."

"Anyway," said Annabel, "none of this helps in finding out who killed Geoff and Ted. It doesn't help in showing *how* Geoff's killer knew he'd be in the dressing-room when he was or that Ted would be alone on the training ground."

No, thought Stu grimly. It doesn't. This weekend we've behaved as if it's all over, but it isn't. Perhaps it's hardly started.

"I'm fed up with talking about it," he said.

So they didn't any more.

*   *   *

There was a letter in Monday's post for Ade Ojokwe. Still on a high after his goal on Saturday, the news in it sent him nearly stratospheric. He was in the Nigerian World Cup squad. At training he was surrounded by congratulating and envious players.

"They should have picked you years ago," said Ronnie. "You're magic. I wish you could play for England."

But hardly had training started than another summons came for Ade. A police Rover drew up outside the training ground and Sergeant Cumberland got out. He approached Wally and spoke softly. Wally's enraged answer was loud enough for everyone to hear.

"What do you want him for? He's got nothing to say. Leave him alone."

Sergeant Cumberland's voice was also raised.

"We want a little talk, just to eliminate him from our inquiries."

Wally, anger showing in every movement, strode over to the players.

"Ade," he said, "they want you. Best do as they ask."

Ade's eyes were wide.

"Me?" he said, surprised. But he pulled his tracksuit bottoms on and left quietly enough with Sergeant Cumberland.

Nicky Worrall nudged Ossie.

"Told you, didn't I?" he said.

Ade's forced departure took a lot of the heart out of training. Wally did his best to gee the players up but without much success. An unspoken thought ran through the whole squad which didn't find expression until they were back in the changing-room.

"I don't believe this," said Ossie Canklow as he unlaced his boots. "I thought it was all sewn up. These murders were because of match-fixing: the police just had to find out who was behind it and it would all be finished. What could Ade have to do with that? He won't even play pontoon."

"So we're not off the hook at all," said Chris Kingdon.

"I don't get it," said Lee Boatman. "Ade was with us all at the time: on the field when Geoff was done in and looking at the model of the stand when Ted fell off his perch."

"But he could have paid somebody," said Kevin. "Like a contract killer. That's how they thought Ted had Geoff murdered."

"That's right," said Nicky excitedly. "That makes sense with Ade. Look how they were both killed. These weren't your boring old bullet-through-the-head jobs. Knife-throwing, garotting – that's way-out stuff."

"What do you mean?" growled Winston.

"You know what the old explorers used to say about these savage tribes in the jungle: all those machetes and blowpipes and poisoned darts. That would be just his scene. He could have got somebody to come over here and—"

"Right, man, that's it," said Winston. He grabbed Nicky under the shoulders and lifted him bodily over his head. "One word more and I take you outside and drop you in the river."

"That'll teach you not to think Sherlock Holmes stories are true," said Lee.

"Sorry, Winston," shrieked Nicky. "I didn't mean—"

"I know what you meant," said Winston grimly, but lowered him to the floor nonetheless.

"All right, cool it, everyone," said Ronnie. "Let's have a bit of sense. No one but a total plonker could imagine Ade had anything to do with this. They've found out there was a bit of bother between him and Geoff and they want to sort it out."

"Yes," said Ossie. "I see that. It means the police haven't got a clue after all so we're still deep in the mire."

"We're not off the hook after all," repeated Chris.

"So which of us is going to be next?" said Nicky.

"You if you don't keep your mouth shut," said Winston.

Just then, Ade walked in.

"I didn't want to miss the photocall," he said.

The questioning had been searching. Ade had not wanted to say what he really thought of Geoff Rundle now he was dead, but Inspector Wagstaffe's insistence had made him express the months of quiet digs, low-voiced taunts, nasty implications.

"But why didn't you tell someone?" said Cumberland.

"I fight my own battles," said Ade. "I have my pride."

"So you wouldn't even tell Winston?"

"Especially not Winston."

"Did you want Rundle dead?"

"Sometimes. But not like that."

"And Ted Rankin?"

Now Ade was really upset.

"Ted was my friend. He helped me as much as anybody when I came here. What happened to him really broke me up."

Wagstaffe and Cumberland looked at each other. They could go no further. This thinnest lead of all snapped in front of their eyes.

"OK, lad," said Wagstaffe. "That's it. You can go."

"And thanks for coming," said Cumberland.

"And for being so frank," said Wagstaffe. "It couldn't have been easy."

*　　*　　*

Back at Louring Park, all Ade's elation had returned. The afternoon April sun shone down. Every player on the staff, plus trainers and physios, was lined up on the pitch in front of the main stand. They sat in four rows, with Wally, George and Ronnie next to each other at the front. Nicky and Ade, the two smallest on the squad, sat at each end of the front row.

"I still say it's a bit tactless to have a photograph now," muttered Ronnie to Wally as they took their places.

"Nonsense," said George, who had overheard. "It's good for morale. If there's a poster of us going all over the country now, it shows no one's getting us down. And just think what it would have been like if we'd had it done last month, with Geoff and Ted still on it. This way we say, 'Nobody shakes us. Business as usual.' Besides, there'll be no more killings."

"Long speech again for him," muttered Ronnie to Winston on his left. "He *must* be worried."

Ade sat bubbling with pleasure. Saturday's game with that marvellous goal, international selection, relief at the outcome of the interview – all swept through him. Life was great – it beckoned him to the very top.

"OK, lads," said the photographer after four takes. "That's it."

They rose up from the chairs, jumped down

from the benches and ran back down the players' tunnel. Except Ade. The photographer packed up his gear and left. The pitch and stands were completely empty. Ade had sat there daydreaming; now as he stood an urge came to take a private lap of honour. He loped across the grass and onto the running track, in front of the North Terrace, round the corner and past the East Stand. Nigeria had just won the World Cup. The German players, humiliated 8-0, lay exhausted and shell-shocked on the ground. Ade had scored a hat-trick. He clutched the trophy in one hand and waved it above his head as the cheering, adoring crowd packing the Los Angeles Rose Bowl roared his name.

"ADE! ADE! ADE!"

"Ade?"

The voice cut into his dream. The crowds evaporated.

"Ade! Look up here." The voice was one he knew.

Ade looked up.

Everybody had changed, but one locker remained unopened.

"Where's Ade?" said Stu.

"Didn't he come in with the rest of us?" said Kevin.

"He can't still be outside."

"He's been in a dream all day."

"We'll look."

So they filed through the players' tunnel out onto the pitch and looked round. When they saw the crumpled heap in cherry red and yellow on the running track under the overhanging roof of the East Stand they rushed across the grass. And when they saw Ade's body, a round hole drilled in his forehead from which blood ran staining the ground, they knew he would never win a World Cup medal with Nigeria.

And it didn't occur to Nicky to call the murder a boring bullet-through-the-head job.

9

A week passed. The whole club was now in deep shock.

After Ade's murder, the same procedure went on as before: the police swarmed all over the place and there was more questioning of everybody at the ground. Once again, every player had a cast-iron alibi. All the rest of the staff who had any business at the ground were accounted for. The spot from which the shot must have been fired was on the roof of the stand. This roof was not a supportless cantilever as planned for the Jim Grundy Memorial: it was supported on pillars and sloped down towards the front to guttering. Flimsy ladders stood at the rear of the stand ready for working on the roof; alternatively (but it was unlikely) the killer could have swarmed up a pillar, to which the downpipes for guttering were attached. There was no trace of anyone having been up there.

"Whoever did this is more agile than a monkey," said Cumberland.

"I'm just not getting a picture," said Wagstaffe. "No idea of what a real suspect may be like. Twenty years I've been in CID and it's not often that's happened. We have a will o' the wisp who knows what everyone's going to do before they do it, and then seems to kill them for fun. Just as you think you're getting somewhere – you've found a motive and an opportunity – then matey gets himself murdered."

"You know what?" said Cumberland. "We're being laughed at."

All the bodies were released that week. On Tuesday, Walter Blyton and Wally Kerns went to Liverpool to represent the club at Geoff Rundle's funeral. On Wednesday, George and Ronnie travelled to Bristol to do the same for Ted. On Friday, all the players lined up at the airport as the coffin containing Ade Ojokwe's body was loaded on to a plane bound for Lagos.

And on Saturday they had to play Millwall at home.

Nicky Worrall, wishing he could bite his tongue out for what he had said to Chris Kingdon the previous week, started a game for only the fourth time that season. For the third match running there was a minute's silence, then the crowd of twenty thousand watched quiet and stunned as the pre-occupied Rangers played like zombies.

Millwall players are not the sort likely to sit back and sympathize, but at least, as Rangers trooped off at the end having been hammered four-nil at home, there were no boos or cries of "What a load of rubbish!" from the fans. Instead a funereal gloom enveloped the ground and the streets around as they drifted away, shepherded by policemen who had no need today to worry about fights with Millwall supporters.

And for the first time since October, Rangers were off the top of the league. One consolation though – City had lost as well and were down to third.

George hurried into the dressing-room at the final whistle. He didn't shout his head off, though the players were expecting it.

"Go home, don't get drunk, have a good night's sleep," he said. "Try to put this behind you. On Monday we pick up the pieces and start again."

So they went home and George went as well, his impassive face not showing the deep stirrings of something in his mind to which he could not yet give a name.

*   *   *

By Monday the mood had lightened slightly. Wally had worked out a few new ploys at dead-ball situations which the players quite enjoyed.

"Next Saturday is crucial," he told them.

They didn't need reminding. Another long journey, this time south to Fratton Park, Portsmouth.

"Pompey can pull the wax out of your ears before you've woken up," said Wally. "It's a terrible place to have to go to when you've *got* to get a result."

But as the morning wore on and the players concentrated on tactics and the game ahead, a spring developed in Rangers' collective step. George and Wally ended it feeling quite hopeful. The atmosphere in the dressing-room afterwards was also lighter. The players could discuss things rationally again.

But there was a difference. They were guarded in what they said. Who knew who was listening? Who knew who might be next?

"What's it all about, then?" said Ossie savagely as he pulled off his boots. "The murders aren't about match-rigging; they're not about race. What did those three have in common to make someone want to do them in?"

"The only thing I can see," said Ronnie slowly, "is that they all played for this club. And that makes me think something that sounds daft, but it's all I can come up with. Revenge."

"On who?" scoffed Nicky. "What had Ade done to hurt anybody? Or Ted?"

"Not on them," said Ronnie, "on us. On the whole club."

There was silence. Then Winston said, "How do you mean, Ronnie?"

"Someone's got a grudge against Radwick Rangers as a whole."

"So they're getting rid of it?" said Ossie derisively. "One at a time?"

"Oh, come on, Ronnie," said Dave Prendergast. "That's daft."

"Of course it is," said Nicky. "What the police ought to do is look for things that changed about the time the murders started. Like who came new to the club."

"Are you saying what I think you're saying?" said Dave.

"You bet," said Nicky. "We were all right till a fortnight ago, then you come in the squad and everything goes wrong. I think the police should have a long look at you."

"You'll never change, Nicky," said Winston.

"You know," said Kevin ruminatively, "there *is* someone I can think of with a grudge against the club. Though it can't mean anything."

"Who?" said Chris,

"Well, I know it sounds daft, but what about Mrs Grundy?"

"Pull the other one!" said Nicky.

"No, listen," said Kevin. "She lost her old man to the club when he was alive. If he followed Rangers all round the country and never missed a home game he couldn't have been at home with her that often. And the pneumonia that killed him he got from standing on the North Terrace in the rain. Radwick Rangers took him away from her and then killed him. She can't be feeling too chuffed about it."

"But she was *proud* of him, for pity's sake," said Lee, "or so the chairman keeps telling us. She brought his ashes in an urn and had them scattered over the pitch. She got herself a job on the strength of it. She's having the new stand named after him. What more can the club do to make it up to her?"

"That's just a publicity stunt," said Nicky.

"I know all that," said Kevin, "but the fact remains that her husband's dead, and if it wasn't for Radwick Rangers he'd still be alive. All the rest is flannel."

"Let me get this straight," said Ronnie. "Are you trying to tell us that Mrs Grundy who serves tea and cakes and never says boo to a goose is a mass murderer who goes round throwing knives at people, garotting them and climbing up on the roofs of stands to shoot them?"

"It's as sensible as anything else anyone's come up with," said Kevin.

"It's *ludicrous*," said Ronnie.

"Well, I don't think so," said Kevin. "I'm going to tell the inspector."

"Suit yourself," said Ronnie. "He'll laugh his truncheon off."

But I'm not laughing, thought Stu. And I'll ask Annabel what she thinks. She won't laugh either.

But she did. Peals of laughter echoed through her parents' house. When they subsided, she said, "All this really must be getting to you."

"It's not my idea. It's Kevin's."

"Well, he doesn't know her, then. Do you?"

"Not really," said Stu.

"She's nice, she's kind, she's quiet. She's put up with a lot in her life and she hasn't complained because that's the sort of person she is. Now, if you'd said Miss Gibson I'd have taken you seriously. She'd wrestle with Rottweilers."

"But the club can't make up for Mrs Grundy's loss, however hard they try."

"Stu, she's *grateful*. She loves her little job and she's thrilled about the stand being named after her husband. There's not an ounce of malice in her."

"Well, Kevin says he's going to the police about it."

"Then I hope they kick him straight out of the door. And if they start persecuting Mrs Grundy,

I'll be round there myself giving them a piece of my mind."

Inspector Wagstaffe didn't laugh. When Kevin had gone he spoke musingly to Sergeant Cumberland.

"What do you think?"

"It's no weaker a lead than any others."

"We've spoken to her already, haven't we?"

"Twice. After the Rundle and Ojokwe murders."

"Why not after Rankin's?"

"Because that happened four miles away at the training ground."

"Hmm." Inspector Wagstaffe didn't seem satisfied.

"Look," said Cumberland, "she's insignificant. She's one of three tea-ladies at the club, out of her depth with all the attention she's suddenly getting. She couldn't do these murders herself and she sure as hell couldn't pay anybody. Going after her would really be clutching at straws."

"We'll bring her in nonetheless," said Wagstaffe.

"You can't," Cumberland remonstrated. "She'd have a heart attack."

"Then we'll go and see her," said Wagstaffe. "Just a casual chat: nothing to draw the attention. Though I do admit that I don't think we'll get very far with her."

"Another wild goose chase," said Cumberland.

"Not entirely," said Wagstaffe. "I don't believe in

the suspect, but I do believe in the motive."

"What motive?"

"Revenge," said Wagstaffe, striding out of the door.

Annabel's cream cakes were late that morning. It wasn't until 11.30, when Miss Gibson was safely in the club secretary's office taking confidential short-hand, that Mrs Grundy sidled up to Annabel with a Bakewell tart and a chocolate éclair.

"I'm sorry I've taken such a time," she breathed. "These two policemen came to see me."

"Whatever for, Mrs Grundy?" said Annabel.

"Just to ask a few questions. They gave me a real turn when they took me on one side. The other ladies were quite taken aback. 'Whatever have you done, Daisy?' they said. But the inspector and the sergeant are such gentlemen, so respectful and polite."

"But Mrs Grundy, whatever did they want to see *you* about?" Annabel said, at the same time think-ing: I'll find that Kevin and I'll *kill* him.

"What my job entailed, whether I get around the place much. Well, I told them, I don't just serve tea to the directors. I try to help everybody, because everybody's been so kind to me. And then they asked me what I thought about the club and Jim and whether I blamed the club that he died so young – he wasn't sixty when he went. Well, what a thing to say! Supporting Radwick Rangers was his great pleasure in life, and if it made him happy then I was happy. And after he'd gone – why, Mr Blyton was so kind and all the directors and Mr Forbes the secretary and Mr Maxton, why, they were all kind too. They're such *gentlemen*, real *gentlemen* every one of them. I'm so happy now, or as happy as I can be without my Jim, so fancy thinking I have a grudge against the club! Why, I owe everything to it. They've done far more than they need for a widow like me."

Annabel was amazed by this speech. She had never heard more than three words at a time before from Mrs Grundy.

"You must have been very upset, having to answer all those questions," she said.

"Of course not," said Mrs Grundy. "I only wish I could have helped a little bit more."

Annabel looked at the worn, innocent face in front of her. There was no guile, no hidden depth in it. She felt a sudden lump in the throat. Poor, put-upon woman, to give up the best part of her life to a football fanatic and then be content with the charity the real object of her husband's passion chose to give her.

But then it made Mrs Grundy happy, so who had the right to criticize?

Miss Gibson strode menacingly out of Mr Forbes's office.

"I'll have to get on with my work," said Annabel. "Thanks for the cakes."

"Don't mention it," said Mrs Grundy, gliding out of the office.

Back at CID Inspector Wagstaffe was pacing the room like a caged lion.

"Blank!" he shouted. "Wherever we go, we draw a blank. I've never been up so many blind alleys in my life."

"Take it easy," said Cumberland. "Something will break soon."

Annabel and Stu were in the Star of India again. Annabel had stopped being angry at the temerity of anyone questioning Mrs Grundy; she was now laughing at Mrs Grundy's effect on her interviewers.

"Well, they've really scraped the bottom of the barrel," said Stu. "I knew Kevin was talking a load of rubbish really."

"But what made Kevin think of her in the first place?"

"It was when Ronnie started wondering what all the victims had in common."

"Like we did?"

"Yes. But all he came up with was that they all played for Rangers."

"That's pretty obvious."

"But then he said that the killer must be taking a sort of revenge on the whole club."

"For what?"

"I don't know. But it was then Kevin came up with Mrs Grundy."

"Just forget Mrs Grundy. What about this revenge idea?"

"Ronnie seemed very keen on it. And he's been around a long time. He's seen a lot."

For the second time a suspicion flashed across Stu's mind. Had Ronnie seen more than they knew?

"Has Ronnie anything in mind?" said Annabel.

"Just a minute," said Stu musingly. "There was all that business about the boss and the story he told us in the coach about Billy Manners. Ronnie was really upset about that: he was there at the time and he told me it didn't happen the way the boss said it did. He said someone grassed on Billy Manners to the chairman, and you could see that for the first time in his life it was crossing Ronnie's mind it might be the boss himself."

"I don't see what that could have to do with it."

"But the boss and Ronnie go way back. The boss brought Ronnie here. Ronnie thinks the sun shines out of him. To find his idol's got feet of clay would be a terrible blow to him."

"Why should blowing the whistle on a crook be wrong?"

"Why lie about it? Why *do* it at all? He could be framing an innocent man. He might have wanted Billy Manners out of the way."

"Why?"

"I don't know," said Stu. "The boss and Manners were supposed to be great mates."

"But what's it got to do with revenge?" said Annabel. "For what? Is someone taking revenge on Mr Maxton? It's a funny way of doing it. He's about the only one who hasn't suffered."

"I know," said Stu. "But all this came because of Ted and the match-rigging, and after Ronnie told me I remember thinking that the two match-fixing affairs were somehow connected. And I was going to ask Ronnie about it. But then Ade was murdered and it went out of my head, because it looked like it couldn't have anything to do with the murders after all."

"But that's the peculiar thing," said Annabel. "Nothing seems to have anything to do with anything else. It's just a maze."

"Ronnie confided in me," said Stu. "I don't think he told anyone else about it." He thought for a moment, then: "Why me?"

"Everyone confides in you," said Annabel. "It's your innocent face."

"I wish they wouldn't," said Stu.

"So let's go and see him," said Annabel. "Talk to him a bit more about it. We could go now."

"I thought we were going to the pictures."

"That can wait."

"So you put Ronnie before Tom Cruise. What's his secret? Anyway. I've got his number. I'll give him a ring as soon as I've finished my coffee."

So he did. Ronnie was in and in ten minutes they were on their way.

10

R onnie lived on his own in a fourth-floor flat in a refurbished warehouse by the river. He had bought it just at the right time: he could sit by the huge double-glazed window, look at the panoramic view and remember smugly how desperate the previous owners had been to sell it to him. A bargain made his unexpected arrival in Radwick all the sweeter.

He had arrived unencumbered by wives or girl-friends. He had left three of the former and innumerable of the latter around the world in his travels – from City to Everton to Spurs to Sampdoria to Atletico Madrid to Hamburg to Middlesbrough to Brighton to Northampton and now back to not so very far from where he'd started. He'd seen and done a lot, had Ronnie. Not only did he feel like a storm-tossed, weatherbeaten ship finally come into harbour – he looked like it as well.

While Annabel drooled over the Swedish furniture ("They sold me that with the flat: I've never known people so keen to get rid. I just beat the bailiffs," Ronnie said proudly), Stu went straight to the glass display cabinet and looked at the medals, the cups and the forty England caps and thought, Will I ever have anything like that?

Ronnie came out of the fitted kitchen carrying a tray with cups and saucers, milk and a jug of fresh coffee. He put them on the glass coffee table and sat back in a black leather armchair while Annabel and Stu faced him on the sofa.

"What can I do for you, then?" he said.

"It's about what you told me," said Stu. "Billy Manners and George. It worries me."

"It worries me as well," said Ronnie.

"Why did you tell Stu and not the others?" said Annabel.

"Because when I look at Stu," said Ronnie, "I see myself at that age. They were strange days for me. My career started off with a real downer that wasn't of my own making. I was disillusioned before I'd even started. Someone I worshipped – my role model, if you like – was no better than a crook. I think that had a big effect on what happened to me afterwards. 'If that's what being a one-club man does for you,' I said to myself after Billy was banned, 'let me wander.' So I did. What's been burning me up these last few days is that my other great hero has got something to hide as well."

"You mean the boss," said Stu.

Ronnie nodded.

"Why would he lie to us?" Stu said. "Have you asked him?"

"Not likely. I've been halfway round the world and got nearly every honour the game can give and I still feel like a little boy in his presence."

"Perhaps his memory's going," said Stu.

"Not his," Ronnie replied. "No, he was completely wrong about how it all came out and he must have known he was wrong. I remember it all now like it was yesterday. An anonymous letter detailing the whole affair was sent to the chairman. He wasn't the sort of person to let things go so he set the investigation up himself. There were no rumours and exclusive scoops in the tabloids like George said, though they had a field day after the story broke. And there's only one reason I can think of for George to lie."

"What's that?" said Stu.

"He wrote the letter himself."

"Why? He and Billy were friends."

"I know. That's what I can't understand. If

George found out he'd have had a go at Billy privately, not shop him. He'd try to find a way out."

"Could George have been in the racket as well?" asked Annabel. "Like thieves falling out?"

"Nothing was ever said to implicate George in it in any way," said Ronnie.

"So if George *did* write the letter, then he wasn't as big a mate of Billy's as you thought."

"But he was," said Ronnie. "They were inseparable. George was always round at Billy's house. George wasn't married then but Billy was the big family man. Adored his wife and little boy."

"Could that be it?" said Annabel. "George fancied Billy's wife."

"Irene? I wouldn't blame him. But he'd get nowhere with her. Rock solid for Billy, she was. No, there's something here I just don't understand."

"And it's all coming to the surface again now," said Annabel. "Is that a coincidence?"

"It must be," said Ronnie. "This is a new generation. History isn't repeating itself. Billy and Irene are in the past."

"So where are they now?" said Stu.

"Billy left his wife, I do know that. She didn't throw him out or anything. He went because he couldn't face her. He probably changed his name. I liked what George said about him coaching young players in faraway places. I sometimes wonder if it might have been Billy who recommended Ade to us."

"If it was," said Stu, "I wish he'd recommended him to somebody else."

"Yes," said Ronnie. "Bad business. All three of them."

"Aren't you scared?" said Stu.

"Why should I be? Whatever bound those three together doesn't apply to me. They were on the way up, I'm on the way out."

"But nothing bound them together," said Annabel. "It's all so random."

"Well, it's got nothing to do with any questions about George nearly a quarter of a century ago," said Ronnie.

They didn't talk about it any more. They sat back and listened as Ronnie held them enthralled with stories of his career.

Ronnie's block of flats was in what was once a rundown area near the junction of the river and the canal. Years before there were docks, then there was dereliction, then there was high-priced restoration. Not all the flats were lived in – the area was quiet in a way Stu hadn't liked when they arrived. As Ronnie talked, he had half an ear concentrated outside. And when he heard a high-pitched tone outside, he said, "That's my car alarm."

Ronnie didn't hesitate. He leapt to his feet.

"Come on!" he yelled and dashed through the door.

Annabel and Stu followed him. The high-security lock on Ronnie's front door clicked behind them. The fast lift purred to the ground floor. They ran into the darkness outside.

No one there.

"Chancers," said Ronnie. "Joy-riders. We frightened them off. You were lucky."

Stu was examining his car.

"Someone's been at the door," he said, "but there's no damage."

He clicked the remote control on his key fob to cut off the alarm.

"They were after the stereo," he said. "It would have been no use to them. It's coded."

"They'd put it in the freezer overnight," said Ronnie. "That unscrambles the code."

"They've gone, anyway," said Stu.

"Don't you be so sure," said Ronnie. "I'm going to have a look. I'm fed up with prowlers round here."

He loped off into the darkness.

"Shall we go?" said Stu. "He can look after himself."

"We can't leave him here in the dark," said Annabel. "We'll have to wait till he gets back."

Standing in the dark was eerie. The murmur of water lapping the river embankment, the gloomy mass of the refurbished warehouse, the quiet of a place which should have been humming with life gave them a chill of fear.

There was no sign of Ronnie.

"Let's go back to the main entrance," said Annabel. "At least it's light there and we can't miss him."

They went back and peered out into what was now a greater darkness.

They waited. No Ronnie.

After five minutes, Annabel nudged Stu and said, "Look over there."

Twenty metres to their right, beside a large Mercedes, an indistinct figure stood. They saw square shoulders, a head bushy with hair, a thick-set body. The figure stalked silently and with athletic movements. As he moved into the half-light, they could see his back was towards them.

"Ronnie?" Stu called tentatively.

The figure showed no sign of having heard.

"He looks unreal," said Annabel.

Stu suddenly caught his breath.

"It's impossible!" he gasped. "I'm seeing a ghost."

"What do you mean?" said Annabel.

"It's Geoff Rundle! What we saw was the spitting image of Geoff Rundle." He shook his head.

"This is sending me round the twist," he said. "Geoff's dead, yet I'd swear I've just seen him."

Annabel gripped his arm.

"Ronnie!" Stu yelled into the darkness.

Thirty metres away, the figure straightened up. He turned and strode towards them. It was Ronnie. Stu laughed with relief.

"It was you all the time," he said. "Why didn't you answer when I called you first?"

"Because these thieves don't always run away," he said. "They hang around the cars – they'll even lie underneath them till they can have another go. I was creeping round having a look."

"Did you know that in the dark you looked just like Geoff Rundle? You gave me a terrific shock."

"I can't say that's a compliment," said Ronnie. "Still, I'll forgive you. Are you coming back?"

"Better be on our way," said Stu. "Thanks for everything."

They got in the car and Stu drove off. Annabel looked behind her and saw Ronnie standing in the light of the main entrance watching them.

"He seems very sure of himself," she said, "but I've got this funny feeling that he's wrong. Deep down. I'm afraid for him."

Stu was turning out into the main road back to the town centre.

"It's amazing," he said. "He looks just like Geoff Rundle from the back. I've never noticed that before."

Suddenly he jammed the brakes on.

"What are you doing?" shrieked Annabel. "You nearly sent me through the windscreen."

Stu looked in his mirror, then did a U-turn.

"We're going back!" he yelled.

He screeched to a halt again outside the flats. They rushed out and into the lift, then hammered on Ronnie's door.

It opened. Ronnie stood there, in loose white jersey and old jeans. In the background they could hear a vintage Beatles album – *Sergeant Pepper.*

"Have you come to finish the coffee?" he said.

Stu suddenly felt foolish.

"I came back to see if you were all right," he said.

"Why shouldn't I be?"

Stu struggled for an answer. But before he made a sound he realized that "Annabel's got this deep-down feeling and I thought you looked like Geoff Rundle" didn't add up to convincing reasons. So why did he feel so uneasy?

"I just wondered whether those toerags who had a go at my car might have tried to get in here as well," he finished lamely.

"No chance," said Ronnie. "Sit down again for a minute."

He went into the kitchen. They heard the noise of a coffee percolator, then Ronnie reappeared with the tray, clean cups and a fresh jug. They realized that he was glad of their company.

"I know," he said abruptly. "Do you remember I told you I'd got highlights on video of that match between City and Burnley that Billy threw? I'll play it if you like. It's worth a look."

Stu saw Annabel's face fall. Despite this, he said, "Love to."

Ronnie owned a huge 90-centimetre flat screen television. A large cabinet by its side contained rows of neatly stacked videos. He peered along them and came to a gap in the row.

"Funny," he said. "It's not there."

"Perhaps you lent it to somebody," said Annabel. She couldn't keep the relief out of her voice.

"No, I didn't," he said.

He paused, puzzled. Then he said, "I'm sure it was here this afternoon. I keep this lot stacked tight together in alphabetical order. And I gave them a dust today. There were no gaps then."

He turned away from the shelves and sat down.

"This is weird," he said. "It's only one of those *Match of the Day* compilations, but I look after my things."

"Do you think somebody *has* been here?" said Annabel.

"No one short of Houdini. Not the sort of people who hide in carparks and set off car alarms," Ronnie answered. "It must be me. Getting absent-minded. Senility beckons."

But they both noticed that for the first time he looked worried.

"Ah, well," he said, "it was a nice idea."

"No more coffee for me, thanks," said Annabel.

"We've got to be on our way," said Stu.

They went back down in the lift, and got into the Peugeot. Annabel sank into the front passenger seat and jumped up again with a cry.

"I've sat on something!"

She felt on the seat and picked up a square, hard object.

"It's a video," she said.

Stu switched on the courtesy light.

MATCH OF THE DAY. Great Games of the 70s.

They stared at it mystified for a full minute.

Then: "Back we go," said Stu.

"Of course I didn't pinch it," Stu roared in frustration. Ronnie was being very obtuse. "I didn't even know it was there. And I'm not so broke I can't afford ten quid in John Menzies."

Ronnie was examining the video. "It's definitely mine," he said. "Here's my address label stuck on the back. So how did it get in your car if you didn't pinch it?"

"I don't know!" Stu was shouting. "If I'd just taken it out of here I wouldn't have brought it straight back."

"You could have taken it to the car and then thought better of it. Or Annabel could have seen what you did and made you bring it back."

"Why won't you believe me?"

"Because what you're saying is impossible."

They looked at each other, mystified.

"Let's calm down," said Annabel. "Let's think sensibly."

So they quietened and they thought. They didn't like what they found.

"There's only one possibility," said Annabel. "Someone came into your flat while you weren't here. And the only time that could have been, if you saw the video in the cabinet this afternoon, is when we were all in the carpark."

"So my alarm was a set-up to get us out of the flat?" said Stu.

"But I've got a ten-lever security deadlock on my front door," said Ronnie. "Who could sort that out in two minutes?"

"Is there another way in?"

"Double-glazed high security french doors to the balcony. I don't see that anyone would shin up a drainpipe in the dark to get to it. There's a fire escape round the side, but a burglar would still have to get in through the front door. Unless of course . . ."

"Unless what?"

"Let's go into the kitchen."

Ronnie's fitted kitchen had a large walk-in larder at one end. A small, hinged, double-glazed window opened out of the far wall.

"I don't remember knocking this down," said

Ronnie, picking up a tin of chopped tomatoes from the floor.

The top casement on the window was open.

"I keep it open," said Ronnie, "but surely it's too small for anyone to get in. And they'd have a scramble up a sheer wall from the fire escape to get to it, or a sheer drop. A gibbon might do it, not a human being."

Stu and Annabel took it in turns to see what Ronnie meant. The metal fire escape was attached to the outer wall. They could see it both above and below the window. Anyone reaching the window from the fire escape would need inhuman agility and nerves of steel.

The three of them walked silently back into the sitting room.

"This is scary," said Annabel.

"Why in God's name has someone gone to such lengths to take a cheap video and put it somewhere else?" said Ronnie.

"Someone who can get in and out of cars with fitted security systems and leave no trace," said Annabel.

"Someone who knows about Billy Manners," said Stu.

There was a pause while the full implications sank in.

"The killer's been here," said Ronnie.

"And he's warning us off," said Stu. "And the

Billy Manners case *is* connected."

"My instinct was right," said Annabel. "You *are* in danger, Ronnie."

"So are you," Ronnie answered.

11

Inspector Wagstaffe now knew that he was getting nowhere. Mrs Grundy had gone and with her the last vestiges of an idea to which he could attach a person.

But the concept, with no person attached to it, lurked stubbornly in his mind.

Revenge.

On who? For what?

No, it couldn't be a personal revenge on Geoff Rundle, then Ted Rankin, then Ade Ojokwe. Nothing held all three together. The betting thing with the first two was a complete red herring. He had spent the week since he let Mrs Grundy out of his clutches re-examining every possibility with betting syndicates and he was convinced that, whatever else they did, they weren't involved in this. Racial abuse? The idea had died with Ade.

"Let's start again," he said to Sergeant Cumberland.

"Where?"

"Let's think about revenge."

"But we've done that already."

"We'll try a different tack. We'll look wider."

"You mean, stop looking for associations between victims?"

"Yes. Let's assume the only connection is that they all played for Radwick Rangers."

"This is bizarre," said Cumberland, "but I'll go along with it."

"Well, what have we got?"

"Opportunity," said Cumberland. "The knowledge that each one would be in a particular place at a particular time. Ted Rankin on the training pitch on his own, Ade Ojokwe at a photocall."

"And Geoff Rundle sent off so he'd be in the dressing-room early?"

"Yes, there it falls down. If it wasn't for that we could assume someone in the know – a player, coach, manager – was priming the killer to be in the right place at the right time."

"Well, let's not get hung up about that. We'll assume it's something we *can* solve and we'll kick ourselves for not seeing it when the truth comes out. Let's think about *revenge*."

Inspector Wagstaffe fixed Sergeant Cumberland with a long, straight look. Cumberland flinched slightly at its intensity.

"This is a deep-laid, well worked out plan," he said. "It involves at least two people: one in the know passing on information, the other some murderous invisible sprite who kills almost at will and disappears laughing at us."

"Just what I'm thinking," said Cumberland.

"But there's no real pattern established yet, so the killings aren't over," said Wagstaffe. "I see no point in killing players one by one till there's none left. There must be a focus, an object, a last victim."

"A grand finale, in fact," said Cumberland. "But who will it be?"

"Anyone from the chairman downwards. Blyton, Forbes, Maxton, Kerns . . ."

"Raikes?" said Cumberland.

"Yes, Raikes," said Wagstaffe musingly. "He's been around a long time."

"Shall I bring him in for a chat?"

"No, not yet. There's plenty at the club who've been there a lot longer. We must have something to go on."

He thought for a moment, then: "There must be personal files on everybody employed at the club. I don't care if they're confidential: we'll see the lot. Get the squad onto it."

"What are they looking for in particular?"

"I wish I knew. We can only tell when we see it. Tell them to watch for any connections over the years between any of the present-day personnel before they came to Radwick. If this *is* revenge we're looking at, then its roots are in the past."

When the coach set off on Friday down the motorway to the M25 and the A3 to Portsmouth, a scene of some chaos was left behind. With Walter Blyton's permission – after the threat of a search warrant if he didn't give it – all the filing cabinets in Miss Gibson's sacred open-plan office were emptied. The contents of drawers were carefully placed in plastic boxes and taken back to CID headquarters. Annabel, puzzled and still disturbed by the events at Ronnie's flat, looked on amazed, but Mrs Grundy cheered her up with a doughnut oozing strawberry jam.

"Don't worry," she said. "I'm sure they'll put everything back in apple-pie order. And they'll soon find this awful murderer."

Annabel wasn't so sure.

The coach was quiet once again. George could do nothing about it. He had played his great motivating trump card on the way to Sunderland and now he sat at the front feeling depression sweep in waves over his head from the seats behind him. Not even a stay in a pleasant hotel overlooking

Langstone Harbour bathed in April evening sunshine could lighten the mood.

"What can you expect?" said Wally in the hotel bar on Friday evening. "Three of the best in the squad gone in a fortnight – I'm surprised the ones who are left turn out at all."

George Maxton was in no mood to agree.

"They're professionals. They've got a job to do. Their reputation's on the line just as much as mine. We *have* to get to the Premiership."

Wally saw a light of fanaticism in Maxton's eyes he had never seen before.

"Steady, boss," he muttered.

Since the night at Ronnie's, Stu had been on edge. An elaborate and dangerous break-in just to move a cheap video from one place to another? It didn't make sense *unless* it was done to scare. Because there did seem to be a message behind it: *Yes, you're right. This is about Billy Manners. You're treading on dangerous ground – stay out.* And was there a postscript: *You're next?*

Ronnie had let him borrow the video anyway, and it now lay on top of Annabel's TV, an object of fear. He had no wish to look at it.

For the following three days, and on the coach, Stu had looked round at his fellow players, his mind beating with frantic speculation. *Which one of you knows more than he is saying? None of you has done the murders, but which of you controls the one who does? Which of you sees this magical fiend every day?* He had a vision of one of his mates – Dave, Ossie, Nicky, Kevin, Winston? – going home to feed his pet, a carnivorous, elastic-limbed monkey with intelligence at genius level. He saw this player, whose face was a blank, shoving tit-bits of blood-stained flesh through the bars, whispering, "This will whet your appetite. Listen carefully to me and I'll show you who your next little playmate is and when he'll be where you want him." And he would whisper in the creature's ear and a ghastly, brutish chuckle would emanate from the creature's mouth as it loped to the back of its cage and rooted among its weapons – knives, nooses, guns: who could tell what other death-dealing objects? Perhaps, next time, just long, knife-nailed, whip-strong fingers? Next time? On Ronnie? On him?

Every night now he woke up shivering from that dream. And every day he looked round and wondered: *Who can it be? Who can it be?*

And something else worried him as well. He dreamt about the killer and he entered the dream each night with another problem: he didn't believe in ghosts, so why should this sudden, laughable idea come to him that Ronnie was Geoff Rundle's ghost? And there was something else – something that meshed in his mind with a fact, a realization which was already there deep in his subconscious.

Something to do with that first Saturday, when Leicester City played at Louring Park and Geoff Rundle ended the match with a knife in his back. Something which, if he could just *think* of it, would start to unravel this whole terrifying business and take fear away for ever.

The hotel terrace overlooked the harbour and Stu stood looking out to sea, thinking he should be savouring this moment in his life. He was part of a potentially great team representing a famous club. He was at the start of what could be a marvellous career. Here he stood, on a calm, azure evening bathed in early summer sunshine, on the eve of a fixture – Portsmouth versus Radwick Rangers – which for eighty years had excited hundreds of thousands of people far away across the country and across the world, glued to radios in ships, riffling through newspapers, scrolling teletext for the result. Yes, he should glory in the moment: it wouldn't come again.

But he couldn't. The fear kept coming back and tearing at his mind.

Ronnie joined him on the terrace.

"You all right, Stu? You look a bit peaky."

"I'm fine," said Stu. "Has anything happened since the other night?"

"Nothing," said Ronnie. "And it won't. No worries, mate."

*   *   *

Fratton Park, Portsmouth, was nearly full. The Milton End was packed with Rangers supporters. The elegant South Stand, the North Stand opposite and the Fratton End shook to the sound of the Pompey Chimes. "Play up, Pom-pey!" filled the air. Portsmouth's royal blue and Rangers' cherry red and yellow glowed in sunshine which told the crowd that the football season was nearly over, its questions all but answered, and soon would come a time for contemplation and regrouping.

But, yet again, this was not Radwick's day. They started well: a move reminiscent of their best days a month before ended with the Pompey goalkeeper tipping a shot from Kevin over the bar and then being beaten by another which hit the post.

"I just don't *believe* Kevin's luck these last weeks," said Wally.

"It'll turn," George replied calmly.

But when the teams trooped off at half-time there was no score and Radwick had more than held their own. George was pleased.

"Do nothing different," he said. "Keep it tight, keep feeding Ronnie and Kevin. The luck will change."

But it didn't.

"I'm changing my boots," Kevin announced. "The studs in these are too long. Anyway, new boots, new luck."

He slipped off the ones he was wearing and put them on, first the left, then the right. Nobody took any notice.

Until the scream filled the dressing-room.

Kevin lay slumped on the floor. His right sock was soaked in blood. The boot he had tried to put on lay on the floor and beside it was a bloodstained razor blade.

His face pale, he stammered out what had happened.

"This blade was in my boot. It must have been put there so I'd stamp down on it. I felt this terrible pain. I threw the boot off at once: the blade didn't go all the way in. It could have cut an artery if it had. I'd have bled to death."

Wally rushed out and called for an ambulance and the police.

Doug Wadsworth and Gus Fame were the substitutes today.

"You're on," said George to Gus.

Radwick Rangers shambled shell-shocked onto the pitch and were beaten five-nil.

The police took statements after the game to send to Radwick. Kevin stayed in hospital overnight. His wound healed fast: he travelled back to Radwick on Monday with crutches to keep his bandaged foot off the ground.

George had said nothing after the game or in the coach. Neither had anyone else – except Stu and

Ronnie, who now sat together.

"Well," said Ronnie, "that's the first time the killer's had a go at a murder and it hasn't come off."

"But it could have," said Stu. "Kevin was really lucky. And how did the murderer know he'd change his boots?"

"Don't get paranoid about this person's capabilities," said Ronnie. "Kevin brings two pairs of boots, like all of us. He's got to wear one of them. Sooner or later he'll wear the other. This was a murder just waiting to happen."

"Only this time it didn't work," said Stu. "But why Kevin?"

"Why indeed? Why any of us?"

The gloom in the coach was such that nobody noticed City had lost as well. For the first time for six months, Rangers and City were not sharing the automatic promotion places. The play-offs loomed, two-legged matches between third and sixth, fourth and fifth in the league and then a final at Wembley for the last of the three promotion places.

12

On Friday and Saturday, CID headquarters was awash with Radwick Rangers files. Wagstaffe had set a huge team to ransack them for details of past contacts. The final collated list was disappointing.

"Rankin and Prendergast started at about the same time at Bristol City," said Cumberland.

"Did they know each other?"

"They must have. But no particular contact that we can see, Prendergast never mentioned it when we questioned him."

"He's new, isn't he?"

"Signed in March, just in time to beat the transfer deadline. Made his debut on the day Rundle was killed."

"So things start happening only after he arrives and when he first plays."

"If he's involved, surely he'd lie low a bit, not get to work as soon as he comes?"

"He's worth another look. Get him in. Anything else?"

"Somerset and Canklow were at Crystal Palace at the same time. Not significant."

"Any other?"

"Raikes was an apprentice years ago at City when Maxton was in his prime as a player. So there's a connection that goes way back."

"As do the roots of revenge," said Wagstaffe.

"But Raikes owes a lot to Maxton," said Cumberland. "He took him off the scrapheap."

"Nevertheless, that's a connection which interests me," said Wagstaffe. "I'd like to see Mr Raikes again when he gets back from the seaside."

"And then there's Kerns and Maxton," said Cumberland. "They've worked together over the years at four different clubs."

"I'll see them both again as well," said Wagstaffe. "But now I'm going to have an evening to myself and a good lie-in on Sunday morning."

But he didn't. Because then the news came of the attempted murder of Kevin Ray.

Night after night now, Stu puzzled over that first death-filled Saturday. What *was* that detail about the Leicester City game that was lodged in a little cabinet at the bottom of his mind and refused to be unlocked?

He stared at the ceiling and went over it yet again.

The Leicester striker burst through with only the goalkeeper to beat.

Ted Rankin was slow off his line, and later confirmed that it was on purpose.

Geoff Rundle rushed over and committed a professional foul to stop a certain goal.

Geoff Rundle was sent off.

Geoff Rundle was murdered two minutes afterwards with a knife hurled deep into his back.

That was it. There was no more. An impenetrable mystery.

So why had a momentary confusion between the dead Geoff and the living Ronnie caused such an electric surge of fear? What had Ronnie got to do with it?

Nothing.

But there had to be *something*. *Something*.

What nugget lay there in the dark? What message remained undeciphered?

"So, a million-to-one chance has prevented the most bizarre murder of the lot," said Cumberland. "I thought a razor blade sticking up in a boot was a pretty chancy way of getting rid of somebody.

Even if it went through an artery, there'd be enough people around to stop him bleeding to death. But this . . ."

It was Sunday. Inspector Wagstaffe wasn't having a lie-in and the two were poring together over the preliminary lab report. There were traces of poison on the razor blade and on the tear in Kevin's blood-soaked sock – Paraquat, a highly concentrated weedkiller. But Kevin's wound had been cleaned and dressed thoroughly.

"If that stuff had got into his bloodstream he'd have had a fairly nasty death," said Cumberland. He'd seen it all in his time, but this made him shudder.

The Portsmouth hospital where Kevin had spent the night was alerted the moment the discovery had been made. But Kevin was showing no ill-effects: he had escaped the poison. The statement taken from him by a local CID man had been received. Already that morning eye-witness statements had been taken from everyone who had been in the dressing-room.

"Let's get the sequence of events right as we've been told them," said Wagstaffe. "Rangers come into the visitors' dressing-room at half-time. Kevin says he's going to change his boots because the studs are wrong. He takes his first pair off, puts his left spare boot on first, stamps down on it and ties it up. Then he puts his right boot on but doesn't stamp. Why not?"

"Because he felt the cut at once. Remember, he's got where he has today because of his lightning-fast reactions and he was sharp enough to stop in mid-stamp, if you see what I mean. If he *had* stamped, that would have been the end of our Kevin."

"OK," said Wagstaffe. "How did our murderer know he was going to change his boots at half-time?"

"He didn't have to. Kevin's bound to put that boot on sooner or later."

"But this murder failed because, through sheer luck and remarkable physical control and split-second reactions, the intended victim doesn't stamp his boots on like he usually does. But the murderer, who obviously knows how Kevin Ray puts his boots on, assumed he would stamp as usual. Do we believe that?"

"I don't see why not," said Cumberland. "I'd doubt it about almost anyone else, but Kevin Ray's special. If anyone can halt a movement in a nano-second, he can."

"Well, if you say so," said Wagstaffe. "So now we've got to see everybody who had access to the team kit before the coach left for Portsmouth."

Stu had been seen early by the police and had said all he knew. Now, on this limpid early summer afternoon as April merged into May, he and

Annabel lay on the grass in their favourite place high in the hills.

He was shuddering slightly.

"It's coming so close," he said, "but where do you look next?"

Annabel placed a soothing hand on his forehead.

"After last Monday, I'd got it into my head it was Ronnie or me next," he went on. "I was going mad waiting for anything strange to happen. Ronnie didn't seem to worry at all. Then *this*! Why Kevin?"

"Why anyone?" said Annabel.

"What are we going to do?" Stu moaned.

"We should tell the police about what happened in Ronnie's flat," said Annabel.

"Ronnie doesn't want to. And anyway, they'd laugh. What crime is there in taking a video from one place and putting it in another?"

Annabel was silent. Then she said, "Why would they laugh if they could see how scared it's made you?"

Stu thought about this for a few minutes. But he didn't answer. It occurred to both of them that there were better things to do on this warm clear day in a beautiful, lonely place than talk about murder.

Wagstaffe and Cumberland were waiting for Ronnie Raikes to be brought in for questioning about his early days with Maxton.

"Say we're right," said Wagstaffe. "These murders are part of a long-drawn-out programme of revenge. What would that tell us about the victims?"

"That they share a guilt for some event in the past that our avenging spirit wants to punish."

"But if there is such shared guilt," said Wagstaffe, "it's beyond us to fathom."

"Too right," said Cumberland feelingly.

"So let's look at it another way. What if we've been wasting our time looking for connections? What if the whole point is that there *is* no connection? What would that tell us?"

"We're looking for a nutcase," said Cumberland.

"But a very clever, very determined and *very, very* angry nutcase," said Wagstaffe. "So angry that usual logic wouldn't apply."

"What do you mean, 'usual logic'?" said Cumberland. "If we've got someone killing at random there's no logic at all. It's just mad."

"The murders are too well set up for that," said Wagstaffe. "There's a pattern all right, but we've got to hunt to find it."

He thought for a long time. Cumberland waited. At last, the inspector spoke.

"Three murders and a near miss in one month as the season ends and Radwick Rangers are within touching distance of their great prize," he said. "What does that suggest?"

"Like I said before," said Cumberland, "a grand

finale. A final victim."

"Exactly. And who will it be?"

"Blyton," said Cumberland without hesitation. "Big man, pots of money, lots of influence, must have made scores of enemies, crackers about the club."

"Oh," said Wagstaffe, slightly nettled. "Well, I'll tell you who I think it is: Maxton. The man who's staked his reputation, so he says, on getting Radwick promoted."

"It'll be one or the other," said Cumberland. "Blyton prides himself on picking Maxton as manager and giving him a free hand – though there's a threat behind it. And Maxton prides himself on handpicking his ideal team."

"So one of Maxton's protégés has got it in for one or other of them. That person, and an accomplice, are playing a sadistic, dangerous game. They've got a plan all right, but it's not a hard-and-fast scheme. They know that you can never paint a scenario and expect it to happen as you want. No, they're cunning, infinitely resourceful and they take their chances with victims who are calculated to cause us the greatest difficulty because we think we can see links which aren't there. I think it's all a path being beaten to either Blyton or Maxton, and it's a terrible revenge being acted out before our eyes. But for what?"

"I'm looking forward to hearing what Ronnie

Raikes has to say," said Cumberland.

Monday. The training ground. On Saturday, the last make-or-break match with Derby County at home. If Radwick won and everyone else in the race lost, there was still a chance of an automatic promotion place in the top two. Anything less and the dreaded chore of the play-offs was certain: a test of character which might well not be passed, the way things were at the moment.

The news was all about Kevin. It was not so bad: a deep cut in his foot, but it was clean. No poison had entered his bloodstream. There was no way he would be fit for Saturday, but he would be there for the play-offs, never fear.

So George Maxton and Wally Kerns did their best to fire their charges up for the coming encounter. But again it was hard. And for the first time George himself was less than wholehearted.

"It's getting to me, Wally," he said when training was over. "I've tried to stay proof against everything and just get on with the game, get on with the job, get Radwick in the Premiership. But how can I watch my lads be cut off one by one? Do you know what I dream at night?"

"No, boss," Wally said doubtfully. Private confessions weren't George's style, yet it seemed he was about to hear the second in a fortnight.

"That I'm in a clearing in the jungle, all on my

own. But there's something – beast or human, I don't know – and it's cutting through the undergrowth: slicing trees, killing everything in its path. And it's coming to get *me*, Wally."

"Careful, boss. We can't have you cracking up."

"Oh, I'll not show this to the lads. But you're my friend and I'll tell you. There's been idle talk about revenge. Well, I think it's true. And the revenge is being taken on me."

"Whatever for, boss?"

"Wally, I wish I knew."

Just for a second, it crossed Wally's mind that George wasn't being quite truthful.

The visit of a police car to the ground on Monday mornings had now become so routine that nobody noticed it and hardly an eyebrow was raised as Ronnie Raikes was asked to go off for questioning.

Mid-afternoon at CID headquarters, and Ronnie had gone. Wagstaffe and Cumberland looked at each other.

"I remember all that happening," said Cumberland. "Why didn't I think of it before?"

"Why didn't Raikes tell us earlier?" said Wagstaffe.

"Why should he?" Cumberland replied. "Do you think there's anything in it?"

"I don't know," said Wagstaffe. "But we'll look

into it. I want you to contact the City police. I want to know if it was a Football Association investigation only or whether the police were involved. I want you to contact the Football Association, newspaper files of the time and the City club themselves. I want every relevant file they've got. It's a long shot but we've got to aim it right. If Maxton did something nasty then, the wheel of fortune may be turning full circle for him at last."

"What did they want, Ronnie?" said Stu.

It was evening and Annabel and Stu stood with Ronnie on the balcony of his flat.

"I told them exactly what I told you," Ronnie answered. "They're really digging up the past and they've spotted that I knew George when he was at City. And it didn't take long to get on to the Billy Manners business. They seemed very interested."

"So it *has* got something to do with the killings."

"It looks like it," said Ronnie.

"Doesn't that scare you?" said Stu.

"Why should it?" Ronnie replied.

Stu nearly came out with a stream of answers, but he thought better of it because in the cold light of day they seemed so silly.

Stu couldn't sleep. That same obsession pounded through his brain. What was that detail on the day of the first murder that would not come to him?

He went through it all again: Geoff's foul, his sending-off, the violent death which awaited him.

But what else? *What else?*

At three, he got out of bed. He went into the kitchen and made coffee. He sat at the table and drank it slowly. A newspaper lay open at the sports page. He idly scanned a football report. It was of a Third Division match, of no importance to him. However, he noticed that the home side won with a goal in injury time, scored by a substitute who had come on the field three minutes before. He looked at the headline: INSPIRED SUBSTITUTION SECURES HOME WIN.

And then his stomach churned inside him and his head reeled. He closed his eyes for a second, then opened them. The headline remained. So did his new insight.

Ronnie should have been substituted that day. But he wasn't because the moment Geoff was sent off George Maxton changed the plan that they all knew about. So it was Ronnie who was supposed to go early into the dressing-room, as he always did when substituted. It was Ronnie the murderer expected. And the murderer, for a moment at most, had thought that Ronnie was the victim, just as, for a split second, Stu had thought Ronnie was Geoff Rundle's ghost.

So Geoff was killed by mistake. It was meant to be Ronnie.

Why Ronnie?

Stu got up from the table. He tiptoed along the hall to the telephone, half expecting the ever-watchful Connie Wilshaw to appear and ask him what he was doing. But to his surprise, because not much escaped her, he was not disturbed. With trembling fingers, he picked up the phone.

"I don't care if he's fast asleep: he's got to know," he muttered to himself.

He tapped out Ronnie's number. He heard the dialling tone at the other end.

Burr-burr. Burr-burr. Burr-burr. Time after time.

"Come *on*, Ronnie," Stu whispered agitatedly. "You're there. I know it. If you'd gone out you'd have left your answer machine on. You can't sleep *that* deeply."

Burr-burr. Burr-burr. Burr-burr.

And then it stopped. Suddenly, as if cut off. Or, Stu realized with sudden relief, as if someone had lifted and gently replaced the receiver without answering. So Ronnie *was* there. The incessant ringing had woken him up but he was too tired (or too preoccupied with other things which, judging from Ronnie's past life, would have something to do with women) to talk.

That was it. Stu went back to bed.

Then – no, this was important enough to *make*

Ronnie pick up the phone. So he came downstairs and dialled again.

Burr-burr. Burr-burr. Silence. Then: "This is Ronnie Raikes speaking. I'm afraid I'm not in right now. But if you'd like to leave a message, please speak after the tone and I'll get back to you as soon as I can."

It's OK, thought Stu. He just forgot to set the machine.

The tone came. "Ronnie, this is Stu. Look, I've just had a thought. It was *you* the killer was after when Geoff was murdered. You were supposed to be substituted and back in the dressing-room early like you always are. But the killer saw Geoff come in and thought it was you. So it *wasn't* random. Why should they want to kill you, Ronnie? It must have something to do with Billy Manners. *Think*, Ronnie. Somebody wanted to shut you up. *Why?* I'll see you tomorrow. Tell me then. Cheers!"

He waited, on the off-chance that Ronnie might hear the message and come at once. But there was no reply. Stu put the phone down and went back to bed feeling happier.

Ronnie wasn't at training next morning. He sent no message. When Wally rang his flat from the training ground the same voice answered: "This is Ronnie Raikes speaking . . ."

Wally's urgent shout of "Move it, Ronnie! Get yourself over here!" had no effect for the whole morning.

"This isn't like him," said George at midday. "I'm going over there."

Throughout training, Stu had been wondering what to do about his revelation of the night before. As soon as Wally dismissed them all for lunch, he was in his Peugeot heading for the police station as George turned his Jaguar towards the river and Ronnie's flat.

Inspector Wagstaffe was there and saw Stu at once. Stu blurted out the lot. Wagstaffe listened carefully, but before he could speak, the phone rang. Wagstaffe listened again, then put it down.

"Right, lad," he said. "You're coming with us."

The Peugeot was left in the police carpark and Stu was sandwiched between two policemen in the back of a large police Rover. Wagstaffe sat at the front. Siren blaring, blue lights flashing, headlamps on, the car raced to the river. In seven minutes they were parked by George's Jaguar outside Ronnie's flat.

George waited at the entrance.

"There's no answer," he said. "The door's locked, there's milk outside and papers in the letterbox. I've shouted through the door – no answer. I don't like it."

A policeman rang the bell, hammered on the door and yelled through the letterbox: "Mr Raikes! Open Up. Police."

Complete silence.

Wagstaffe nodded.

The policeman shoulder-charged the door. With its high security lock, this was hard. At last, though, it cracked and gave way.

The flat was quiet and so spotless that the policemen moved round it almost reverentially.

"In here," came a voice from the bedroom.

Wagstaffe entered, followed by Stu.

Ronnie appeared to be asleep in bed, his head resting on a red pillowcase.

But he was not. He had been shot through the head at close range and had probably not been aware that anyone else had been in the room.

13

"Catch him," said Wagstaffe.

A policeman caught Stu as he fell.

But Stu wasn't going to allow himself to be sat in a chair and brought round. He was ashamed of fainting, but he wasn't ashamed of the grief which flooded in with the shock. Ronnie had changed fast from childhood hero to good friend, and Stu's loss was personal.

The police combed the flat.

"Larder window open, sir," a voice called.

Stu cranked his brain into action. The larder window had been open once before. That was how the intruder had come and left the night the video was removed.

"Inspector Wagstaffe," he said, "I've got something to tell you."

Wagstaffe listened.

"I wish you'd told us all that before," he said irritably when Stu had finished, "but thanks, anyway."

Stu watched as the forensic team and the police surgeon arrived.

"Time of death?" asked Wagstaffe.

"About two or three in the morning, I should think," said the surgeon.

About the time I rang, thought Stu.

Then something like a cold fist gripped his heart.

It must have been the murderer who replaced the receiver. It must have been the murderer who switched on the answering machine.

Then – worst realization of all – the murderer probably sat down and listened with the greatest interest to Stu blurting out how Geoff had been killed by mistake and Ronnie was the intended victim.

"Inspector Wagstaffe," he said again, this time in a weaker voice.

Once again the inspector listened. Then, this time with no trace of irritability, he said: "Thanks, lad. You've established the time perfectly for us. And don't worry – I know you think you've put yourself in danger, but we'll keep an eye on you."

I bet they will, thought Stu. They know the next victim.

A thought occurred to him.

"Inspector," he said, "why should the murderer

let me know he's there by putting the receiver down? Wouldn't he have got out quick and let it ring? He only draws attention to himself."

"I sometimes think this one *does* want to draw attention to himself," said Wagstaffe. "All this time we've just been laughed at. I tell you, this killer's getting right up my nose."

Back at CID, Wagstaffe spoke to Cumberland.

"We've made a huge omission in only seeing Raikes," he said. "We've got to talk to Maxton again. I'm beginning to think this Manners business is at the heart of it all."

Cumberland had found out a lot.

"It was certainly a big affair," he said, "but as far as I can see there's no letter on file at City that shopped Manners, no matter what Raikes told us."

"That's why I want Maxton's version," said Wagstaffe. "Where are Manners and his family now?"

"Interesting," said Cumberland. "There's a report that Manners changed his name and went abroad. He certainly left his wife and kid. She's dead. She died in a fire five years ago. Her son identified her."

"So she's out of the running," said Wagstaffe.

"Irene Manners was a remarkable woman, by all accounts. Daughter of a showman, brought up in a circus – not the sort to settle down, you'd have thought. But she and Billy Manners were an inseparable, devoted couple it seems."

"Yet it all ended messily," said Wagstaffe. "Where's the son now?"

"No idea. Last heard of two years later in America. Philadelphia."

"Joined his father?"

"Could be."

"We must find out. Get on to the Philadelphia police. Meanwhile, I want to see Maxton."

Annabel was distraught and Stu spent a lot of time comforting her.

"I liked him so much," she said. "He was wise. I want you to be like him."

In spite of his own distress, Stu was pleased. It was good to hear Annabel praise Ronnie; and he was glad that she thought of him as cast in the same mould.

A stunned grief settled over the town of Radwick as well as the football club. But at a press conference, Walter Blyton insisted there was no question of Saturday's match being postponed.

"Why not?" demanded an angry Ossie Canklow at training. "We're in no state to play."

"In 1958, Manchester United beat Sheffield Wednesday in a 5th-round cup replay ten days after the Munich air disaster," Wally answered. "So stop snivelling and get your boots on, lad."

Maxton had left CID. Once again, Wagstaffe and Cumberland were on their own.

"He didn't give much away," said Wagstaffe.

"On what I've got, his version's just as likely as Raikes'," said Cumberland. "We just have to get that tip-off letter Raikes was so insistent on."

They had no idea how troubled George Maxton was and what ghosts of long-dead miseries were rising to haunt him.

Ronnie's funeral was a huge affair. Everybody who was anybody in football was there, including representatives from the clubs he had played for in Italy, Spain and Germany. The streets of Radwick were lined three deep as the hearse passed through from church to cemetery. Stu was overwhelmed by it all.

"Is this how I'll go?" he muttered to Annabel at the cemetery.

"Well, it's something to look forward to," she answered.

Stu smiled. But there was no answering smile in her eyes, and he knew why. His heart sank again, as it so often did now. Because he was the next victim. He knew too much.

The funeral was on Friday. On Saturday was the vital last game at Louring Park. The day was fine, the ground was packed, but the atmosphere in the May sunshine was muted and sad.

No Kevin. Doug Wadsworth, eighteen and a promising young striker out of the reserves, took his place. Gus Fame kept his in midfield. So now only Rick McBain from Connie Wilshaw's hadn't yet made the first team. The teams lined up before the kick off – Derby in their white shirts and dark blue shorts, Radwick in the familiar cherry red and yellow – for a minute's silence. Stu reflected that, apart from the first, every game he'd played for Radwick had started with a minute's silence and had entailed the wearing of a black armband.

The game, when it finally started, was a farce. Radwick played like haunted zombies, like men in shock. Delighted Derby forwards rattled in five goals. This comprehensive home defeat was one goal worse than the previous hammering by Millwall. Since the point at Sunderland, Radwick had soaked in fourteen goals, scored none and lost three games on the trot, had sunk to fourth in the league and looked doomed to another season in the First Division.

Nobody said a word in the dressing-room afterwards. George and Wally came in, muttering "Bad luck, lads. You'll pick up," "It's the same for all of us," and the like. They lightened no spirits: everybody was lost in his own private thoughts.

Then Kevin swung into the dressing-room – still on crutches, with his bandaged foot clear of the ground and a broad smile on his face.

"Don't worry," he shouted. "This will pass. And I'll be back for the play-offs. I'll score six. Just forget your misery and look forward to Wembley."

It wasn't as easy as that. In a week's time it would be the Cup Final. Radwick had been dumped out in Round 4 by Ipswich Town: the final at Wembley might rivet the rest of the country but this year no one in Radwick could care less. Then on Saturday it would be the first play-off match – at home to Wolverhampton Wanderers. On Wednesday would be the second leg at Molineux – not the most inviting of venues for a visiting team – and the winners would go to Wembley to meet the winners of the other play-off semi-final on the following Bank Holiday Monday.

So there was a week to recover shattered morale.

"We've got to make the most of it," said George to Wally.

Sergeant Cumberland had been thinking.

"Sir," he said to Wagstaffe as they pored over relics of the Billy Manners affair and grew no wiser, "are we sure we're not chasing another shadow? The wife's dead, the father and son have disappeared – the whole thing's finished, surely."

"You heard from Philadelphia, then?" said Wagstaffe.

"Not a trace of him," said Cumberland.

"How can we be sure of anything?" sighed Wagstaffe.

"We've been looking for contacts in the past and we came up with Raikes and Maxton at City. As soon as we speak to Raikes, he gets killed."

"Which suggests we're on the right lines," said Wagstaffe.

"Except that we thought we were on the right lines with Rankin and he gets killed; on the right lines with Ojokwe and so does he. Ray comes to see us with information: now he's lucky to be alive. Look what's happened to Raikes. It's like our interest in any suspect is his death sentence. So perhaps we're wrong. Perhaps the killer *wants* us to follow these cold trails. Perhaps we should be looking much nearer home."

"Go on," said Wagstaffe.

"Well, we wanted contacts in the past. I'll show you a contact in the past which has gone on being a contact and is still there, right in front of our eyes."

"Being?" said Wagstaffe.

"Maxton and Kerns. They've worked together for years: Radwick's their fourth club. You might say one's no good without the other. Like they used to say about Brian Clough and Peter Taylor.

Then they split up and Cloughie did marvels on his own."

"I don't see what you're getting at."

"Maxton's top dog: he's always got the best job. What might Kerns feel? Resentment? Jealousy? Frustration at never being the big man with the fame and glory? Wally Kerns, the little fellow behind the scenes. Perhaps he's fed up. Perhaps the worm has turned. Perhaps *he's* taking the long revenge against the man who's stolen his thunder, who takes the credit but can't do without him."

Wagstaffe was silent.

"It would solve a lot of problems for us," insisted Cumberland. "And it fits. We looked for someone who knew everyone's movements in advance: here he is. Kerns kept Rankin back for extra training; Kerns arranged the photocall; Kerns has access to all the team kit. Kerns is ideally placed to work with our unknown accomplice."

Wagstaffe stroked his chin. "So you think it might be the break-up of the dynamic duo," he said. "Clough and Taylor, Morecambe and Wise – every partnership is doomed in the end."

"That's it exactly," said Cumberland.

"Like Wagstaffe and Cumberland?"

"I never said that, sir."

"I know. But you might have something here. I like it."

"So shall I get Kerns in?"

"Not with our track record lately. No, let them have a rest for a while. They deserve it. We'll just keep a close eye on him."

On Tuesday, the whole first team squad, with George and Wally, took off in a charter plane from Radwick Airport for Gran Canaria for a hastily arranged four-day break in the sun. Wagstaffe and Cumberland gave permission for them to leave the country, but three plain-clothes policemen found themselves having an unexpected holiday keeping watch.

Kevin flew with them, his foot nearly healed. The other players regarded him almost in awe, like a visitor back from the dead. In the sun, his wound did its final healing. Far away from home, free of reporters and TV interviewers, safe and watched over, the team's spirits lightened. The weight of fear and misery gradually lifted from their shoulders and instead came determination, a collective will to win through the play-offs. It was the best and only thing they could do for Geoff, Ted, Ade – and most of all for Ronnie, their captain, inspiration and proof of what their chosen sport had to offer.

So the confident band of people who stepped into the arrivals lounge on Friday evening was far different from the shambling rabble who had stumbled aboard the plane on Monday. George and Wally congratulated each other.

But four days in the sun had not exorcised the newly-risen ghosts in George's mind.

As soon as he was out of the airport and on his way to Annabel, Stu felt fear return. He was marked; he was watched; he *knew* it. He drove with one eye on his rear-view mirror: who was following him? When he got out of his car and locked it, he stole furtive glances all round before he dashed up Annabel's drive to the front door. When she opened it, he cursed himself for irrational stupidity.

But it was so good to be back. He resolved that the last thirty-six hours before the first play-off match would be spent shut away from the world with Annabel.

They didn't even go out that night. They sat in front of the television.

"But there's nothing worth watching," moaned Annabel.

"We could rent a video," said Stu.

"We've got a video you haven't watched yet," said Annabel. She produced Ronnie's *Match of the Day* video, still with its address label on the back. In all the recent tribulations, Stu had forgotten it.

"What do you want to see that for?" he said. "You hate watching football."

"It was Ronnie's," said Annabel.

"Oh, heck!" said Stu. "I should have taken it to the police."

"Too late now," said Annabel.

So they watched it: a compilation starting with grey ghosts flitting round the screen, then changing to garish colour and long-haired men with sideburns, wearing round-necked shirts.

Then – 1971: Burnley v. City.

Stu caught his breath. "Of course! This is the match that Billy Manners threw. Remember what Ronnie said? Nobody would have suspected him, but if you know what to look for you can see how he does it."

He watched keenly. Burnley's first goal came up. City were working the ball away from their penalty area. A tall, elegant figure in City's all-white came away with the ball. He slowed and looked round. He seemed to have all the time in the world for all the frenzied movement around him.

"Billy Manners," breathed Stu.

Then, before the inevitable Burnley tackle, he swept a long, raking pass out to the right, aimed, it seemed, for the City right winger. But it didn't reach him: the Burnley number 6 cut it out and started an attack which Billy raced back to defend against. He won the ball again and played it square to his number 8. But the pass was intercepted: the ball was hammered into the back of the City net. Burnley players fell over themselves with joy: Billy spread his hands in an "I did my best" gesture.

Stu stopped the video, rewound it and watched again.

"Marginal," he said.

He watched a third time.

"It could be," he said. "Each decisive move came from a misplaced pass from Billy Manners. The thing is, was he good enough to *mean* them to be misplaced passes?"

Burnley's second goal was coming up. They had a corner and Billy was back to defend. Over came the ball: heads went up. Billy towered above the rest. He headed it clear – straight to the feet of the number 9 who volleyed through a crowd of players. The camera panned round a Turf Moor crowd incredulous with delight.

Stu shook his head.

"If Burnley could take their chances like that, how come they went down to the Fourth Division?" he said.

He watched it again.

"If Billy Manners engineered those two goals deliberately then he was a genius," he said.

"Ronnie said he was," said Annabel.

The last goal. Billy again came away with the ball. This time he actually stopped, put his foot on it and looked round.

"You don't *do* that," shrieked Stu. "Not unless you're God or you want to get clattered."

He was clattered. The ball was taken off him as

he stood there weighing up the options and ten seconds later the City goalkeeper was fishing the ball out of the net.

"That I *do* believe," said Stu.

The last highlight was coming up. City had a penalty. Billy was to take it. He placed the ball on the penalty spot with great deliberation. He stood over it for some time, staring hard at the Burnley goalkeeper. Then he walked back six paces, stopped, pulled his socks up and adjusted the knot in his right boot. He ran up, sent the goalkeeper the wrong way to the left, and hit the inside of the right-hand post. The ball ran tantalizingly across the front of the goal. A Burnley defender charged up and hoofed it into the crowd.

"Can anyone *mean* to hit a post?" cried Stu.

He watched it again.

And again.

And again.

"Must you keep doing that?" said Annabel.

Stu didn't answer for a moment. Then he stopped the video.

"There's something about the way Billy Manners moves. Mannerisms, actions – I *know* them. He reminds me of someone."

"Who is it?"

"I don't know. But it's someone close. Who? *Who?*"

14

Sunday was cold and cloudy – heavy rain in the morning, the afternoon grey and dark.

The weather matched the mood of the whole of Radwick. Louring Park was packed. For the last time, the North Terrace was filled with standing spectators; the demolition firm was ready to start on Monday so the foundations of the Jim Grundy Memorial Stand could be laid. A few regular fans staged a demonstration against the terrace's demise, but police soon cleared them and the rest of the crowd neither cheered nor booed. The stadium radiated no anger, no joy, no wild enthusiasm – just a quiet, intense, sympathetic preoccupation.

The teams came out, Wolves in their old gold shirts and black shorts, Radwick in the usual red and yellow. They kicked off to a hard, dour struggle which matched the weather. Radwick played with a careful concentration, eliminating mistakes. Ronnie's flair was missed. Rick McBain was in and Connie Wilshaw was in the stand screaming encouragement to her lads. Rick was a good player all right, but not the same. Stu, with seven first-team games behind him, looked at Rick and felt a hard-bitten veteran. But it was good to have Kevin back. The crowd gave him a huge reception and in return – as if to show that he didn't depend entirely on Ronnie – he gave a hard-working display which brought its reward in the second half.

Chris Kingdon cut out a cross from the right and rolled the ball to Winston. Winston found Stu, who carried it forward, exchanged passes with Gussie Fame, worked the ball out to the right and crossed low and hard. Kevin took the ball with a neat, economical movement on the turn and cracked it past the Wolves goalkeeper. It was Kevin's first goal since the day Geoff Rundle was murdered.

The crowd's roar sounded a note of relief and thanksgiving as well as joy. There *was* hope: events hadn't destroyed the spirit of the team.

That was the only goal. Would it be enough for the second leg on Tuesday evening?

It was. Molineux saw another grim struggle.

Radwick had travelled to defend what they had gained, and somehow they did it. No goals. Chris Kingdon was voted man of the match.

For the first time in weeks there was a contented dressing-room afterwards.

"Who've we got at Wembley, then?" shouted a happy Nicky.

Wally had been listening to his transistor radio.

"Would you believe it?" he said. "City."

Who would have believed it indeed? Fate had decreed that George Maxton's past and present were to meet to decide his future.

On the coach back to Radwick, Wally spoke to George.

"Nearly there, boss. Mission all but completed."

"I said I'd stake my reputation on promotion," replied George. "And I meant it."

Inspector Wagstaffe was thinking.

"There's something so blatant about the way our killer works," he said. "I'd bet a year's salary that he's got a grand finale in store for us at Wembley on Monday."

Cumberland nodded. He'd thought so too.

"And I reckon Kerns will be behind it. Why won't you bring him in?"

"Because if you're right, I don't want to alert him. And if you're wrong – well, you know what happened before. I don't want him dead."

Cumberland wasn't going to let his theory go without a fight.

"Just a minute," he said. "Forewarned is forearmed. The only pattern we have is that anyone we question ends up murdered. We've already got young Stu and Mrs Grundy to keep an eye on. So we get Kerns in. We either eliminate him or we go for him."

"I don't like it," said Wagstaffe.

Cumberland tried again.

"We see him, then we keep him under close surveillance at Wembley. We can't lose. He's either a prime suspect or the next victim."

"The predator or the bait," said Wagstaffe.

"Right, boss!" said Cumberland delightedly.

Wagstaffe thought for a moment.

"Yes," he said at last. "I like it. Close surveillance on Mr Kerns. Wembley, here we come!"

Five days for Stu of kaleidoscopic feelings. Annabel in every waking thought and most sleeping ones as well. Incredulity that in seven weeks he had gone from obscure reserve to an appearance at Wembley. Some players could go through their whole career and not have that. Grief for loss of friends: Geoff, Ted, Ade, especially Ronnie. Underlying everything, fear – that he was next because he knew too much. Malevolent eyes, he was sure, followed his every movement. But whose?

Sometimes this mix of emotions cleared like rising mist, revealing another layer of difficulty. Billy Manners' movements, his lithe grace, his distinctive actions, flitted across his mind as if on a big screen. And he *did* know them. They were close. But who was it! *Who*? That single pronoun beat a tattoo in his brain until his head ached as he tried to dig deep for the second little nugget of hidden truth.

Annabel worked hard in the office during those last few days before Wembley. Not only did she have to organize the paperwork behind the sale of tickets to fans queuing outside the ground throughout the week, but she also had to make the arrangements for special parties. One in particular concerned her. She told Stu.

"Mr Blyton's organized a special luxury coach," she said. "It's for him, the directors, the president of the Supporters' Club and a few other special guests. Guess who they are."

"Not a clue," said Stu.

"I'll tell you four of them," she replied. "Mrs Grundy is Mr Blyton's personal guest."

"I'm not surprised," said Stu. "He's gone over the top on that gimmick."

"She's so pleased it's pathetic," said Annabel. "She's more like the club mascot every day."

"And the others?" said Stu.

"Miss Gibson."

"That old trout?"

"She deserves it. She's not so bad. She works hard."

"Who else?"

"Your Mrs Wilshaw."

"That I do agree with. She puts up with a lot from us. There's one more. Who is it?"

"Me."

"*You?* Going to a *football match?*" Stu couldn't believe it.

"Mr Blyton thinks it's a reward for me. Well, I'll enjoy the food, anyway. And Mrs Grundy said she wanted me with her as her companion."

"Why you?"

"She likes me. Remember, she gives me cakes. She said if I didn't go she wouldn't either. Moral support in a male world."

"You'll need it," said Stu. But deep down he was pleased.

While fans queued for tickets outside Louring Park, training sessions at the practice ground were intense. George tore into the team with furious concentration.

"This has really got him going," observed Wally Kerns.

Indeed it had. Wally didn't know what was happening to George. He'd been calm, aloof, stern all this time: his great confession on the coach had been for the players, not for himself. But, like a monster at the bottom of the sea stirring after years of sleep, memory was causing strange currents and eddies in his mind. He used to sleep soundly every night, but now ghosts he only dimly recognized stalked his mind. An obsession was growing: this match at Wembley was his destiny in more ways than just clinching promotion.

And they were to play against City, of all teams! George knew that when City strode onto the pitch, in their so-familiar all-white strip, he would see the ghost of Billy Manners stride with them.

"Are you OK, boss?" Wally Kerns asked. He was shocked at Maxton's red-rimmed eyes and unshaven face.

"Tension. It's getting to me at last," George answered.

"It's not like you," said Wally.

Not for the first time, Wally reflected that he didn't know his long-term colleague as well as he thought. Wally let nothing bother him. He hadn't worried about being hauled in front of Wagstaffe and Cumberland for a couple of hours. He'd told them nothing they wanted to hear: back at the club, everyone seemed to think his interview was a joke. Wally agreed. Best for him to be left alone to get on with his job, he thought.

He knew all about City's play. He'd studied

them, watched videos, been to see them. He'd worked out tactics and dead-ball ploys a-plenty and Thursday and Friday were spent perfecting them. After training on Friday, George took over and spoke to the whole team.

"This game is tough," he said. "Winner takes all. If we lose we may not get another chance for years. It will be tight: it may go to penalties."

There was silence. Radwick Rangers had never been in a penalty shoot-out before.

"I hate penalties," said Dave Prendergast.

"They're exciting to watch," said Nicky.

"They're a rotten way to decide promotion," said Wally. "But those are the rules. We've got to have a strategy, a definite order of who takes them, so if it does happen there's no panic and we'll all know exactly what we're doing."

The players settled down to hear Wally's decision.

"Kevin first: he's the hottest shot. Then Winston: he's so calm he'll take it in his stride. Then Lee. Then Nicky. Then Ossie. First five. If it's not over by then, Stu takes the sixth. Then Dave."

Stu didn't know whether to be relieved or not. The contest *should* be over by the end of the first five penalties; if more were needed the tension would be unbearable.

Then Kevin spoke.

"Wally," he said, "why not put me on fifth?"

"Why?" said Wally.

"Psychology. City will expect me first. They won't like it if I'm being saved up till last: it'll unsettle them. And no disrespect to Nicky and Lee, but we may *need* our fifth penalty to count."

"Good thinking, Kevin," said Wally. "I like it. That's what we'll do."

On Saturday the team coach set off down the M1 with two extra passengers on board. If it were not for the revolvers they carried, the two plain-clothes policemen would have thought they were on the best surveillance duty of their careers. Walter Blyton's coach followed. By early evening they reached the Noke Hotel, south of St Albans and just off the M25. Now Stu was forced to spend an abstemious night with the team while Walter Blyton's party had a great time in the restaurant and lounge.

But he wouldn't have wanted it any other way. The shared feeling of single-minded concentration that came with the start of the play-offs was stronger than ever: release and celebration were still a whole day away.

An early night, a light work-out in the morning and then back in the coach and a gentle ride through north-west London until the white bulk of Wembley Stadium topped by its twin towers made stomachs knot with fear, and feet tap in an urgent wish to get on the pitch and start playing.

Everything else was forgotten. The last months had led to this moment and no other.

All morning the cars and coaches had pounded down the motorway. Red and yellow scarves fluttered out of windows which bore slogans ranging from the simple "Rangers for Promotion" or "City Coming Back" to the obscure "Klassic Kevin Kauses Kaos", which only a true supporter would understand. And now Wembley was all but full, one end a field of red, the other a sea of white. This was no big society occasion: the Royals had had their fill of football the week before at the Cup Final. This time it was Walter Blyton who led his party into the Royal Box, along with Football League officials and his City counterparts. "Queen for a day," Stu had said to Annabel, and as she sat with Miss Gibson, Mrs Grundy and Connie Wilshaw on seats cushioned in red velvet on which famous people had sat over the years, just for a moment she believed it.

Then she saw Inspector Wagstaffe and Sergeant Cumberland behind her and reality interposed. She knew that policemen dressed as supporters or stewards were everywhere, as well as the usual very visible ones in uniform. A tiny shiver ran through her. This was not just a football match – something might happen on this the last day of the season, and then more questions would be answered than who was to be promoted to the Premiership.

Radwick were in the South Side dressing-rooms – the lucky dressing-rooms which Don Revie had commandeered for England's perpetual use years ago, giving in to superstition as well as undeniable fact. Stu had entered and seen his kit ready – his number 4 shirt hanging from its peg, his shorts and socks neatly folded on the bench. Tension was high. The players changed with slow deliberation. Socks were pulled up with elaborate care, boots tied and retied to precise tightness. The England shield on the wall brooded impassively over them. Chris Kingdon threw a football over and over again at Peter Shilton's rebound board. "Give it a rest, Chris," shouted Nicky when he could stand the noise no more.

Then George spoke.

"Right, lads. Everything has led up to this day. You've had a time which no one should have to endure. You've been marvellous to get through it. I have complete faith in you. Play your usual game the way you know best. Remember: you'll win today for me, for yourselves, but most of all for everyone out there."

The silence broke as Nicky Worrall laughed.

"Boss, don't tell us it's for the Mrs Grundys of this world and their husbands."

George's face relaxed into a smile.

"No, Nicky, I won't. But you must admit, the chairman's got a point."

Kevin laughed too, then Lee, then the rest.

The bell rang.

"Time, lads," George said.

So out they trooped: George leading, then Winston as captain, Chris, Nicky, Kevin, Lee, Stu, Dave, Ossie, Gus, Doug and Rick. They stood in a line on the left side of the tunnel. Wind blew down the slope in front of them; beyond its horizon they could see bright sunshine and hear the crowd's roar. They knew that virtually every great player in the world had stood where they now stood, and the knowledge knotted their stomachs but swelled their chests with pride.

"I'm here," said Stu aloud. "I've arrived."

City, in white, stood by them. Officials first, then managers, they started the long walk forwards into the glare and noise of the giant greenhouse of Wembley Stadium. And along with them, they were sure, walked the shades of Geoff, Ted, Ade and Ronnie, to wish them well and to be with them at the end of a long campaign.

George's feelings as he walked beside the City manager were too deep to express. Seeing the line of players all in white – those colours which had meant so much to him and had cast his whole destiny – he remembered Luke Jackson, hero of his youth. He knew this would be a pivotal day in his life, one which would define his existence.

Taking his place with Wally Kerns on the benches at the end of the Royal Tunnel, he looked up at the Royal Box, where he could make out the faces of the Radwick party. Some managers would have joined them, but today the suit was left behind. His place was with the team and his garb was a tracksuit. The days of aloofness were gone.

In the noise of the crowd, Wagstaffe and Cumberland could talk to each other but not be overheard.

"Can you see our people?" muttered Wagstaffe.

"Oh, yes," said Cumberland. "The Met and the stadium staff have been very co-operative. I've got six watching Maxton and Kerns and the rest dotted everywhere looking for anything out of the ordinary. That's besides the usual police and staff on duty. They all know what to do."

"So we wait for things to happen," said Wagstaffe. "What do you think it will be?"

"No idea. Something. Perhaps Kerns will make a move soon."

"Or be moved against."

"Not if this affair's going to last beyond George Maxton's big day."

"Hmmm," said Inspector Wagstaffe, not for the first time.

In spite of herself, Annabel was excited by the green of the pitch, the colour, the noise, the – she looked for the word – *ritual* of it all. She sat between Miss Gibson and Mrs Grundy. Miss Gibson said nothing but surveyed the scene with pursed lips. Mrs Grundy, sitting in the end seat with her umbrella propped against the wall across the gangway, leaned over to Annabel and said, "Isn't it all lovely?"

You'll never change, you two, thought Annabel, settling to watch the game.

The preliminaries were over. Winston and the City captain tossed up. Winston lost: the teams changed ends. The referee looked at his watch, signed to his linesmen, looked at his watch again.

The teams were ready. The referee blew his whistle. The match was on.

15

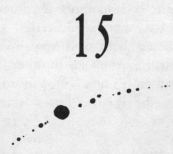

As soon as Stu's feet touched the grass on the Wembley pitch he knew this was to be an experience that would live with him for the rest of his life. The feel of the tight, springy turf, the crowded stands, the brooding presence of the beflagged twin towers – all filled him with a mixture of unforgettable sensations. He would savour every second to the full.

There was still tension in the Radwick team. In the second minute Winston, of all unexpected people, pushed the ball tamely to the City number 9 and Chris Kingdon did well to turn the shot round the post. Five minutes later Lee Boatman was caught in possession. How the City number 8 lifted the ball over the bar from three yards defied explanation.

Nothing went right. The fans at the Radwick end were subdued as if waiting for the inevitable. Five minutes before half-time it came. The City goalkeeper cleared deep into the Rangers half. Gus Fame headed the ball forwards and Nicky failed to reach it. The City number 7 started a run down the right, crossed hard and low. Winston was beaten to the ball by the City number 9, who shot on the turn and gave Chris Kingdon no chance.

One down. The Premiership was receding fast over the horizon.

"You're not here to watch the match," Wagstaffe reminded Cumberland at half-time.

"But there's nothing else happening," the sergeant answered. "Kerns hasn't left his place except to jump up and down and wave his arms about. Maxton's stayed still as a rock. Stu Burton's hardly been threatened by a City player, let alone a murderer. Mrs Grundy's safe in her seat in front of me minding her own business. As an operation, this is a complete dead loss so far."

He sat gloomily back in his seat as the military band thumped and blared its way across the pitch for the third time.

George Maxton did not shout at the Rangers players when they stumbled dejectedly back to the dressing-room. For a moment he surveyed them as they sprawled wearily on the benches, then he spoke, gently but firmly.

"You can do it," he said. "They're not that good. They're nowhere near the City I knew. You have the beating of them. Believe in yourselves. Believe in me. Today is *our* day."

There was silence. Then Kevin said, "I'll score today, boss. I know it."

"So do I, Kevin," said George. "So do I."

He left the dressing-room. All the players saw how slowly he walked, bowed like an old man in a tracksuit. They were shocked into silence.

Wally broke it.

"Forty-five minutes to decide our fate," he said. "Let's go."

For Annabel, the day was proving one of more and more surprises. She was actually *enjoying* the game. The buzz, the passion in the stadium, the almost geometrical movements of the players on the luminous green pitch worked in her mind even more than the actual events. But she was always aware of one figure in particular out of the twenty-two as Stu – dark, stocky, neat in his movements, trim in red and yellow shirt and shorts – crossed and recrossed her vision. At the same time she was aware of the three women beside her – Connie Wilshaw excited, screaming as if she were on the terraces with rattle and banner; Mrs Grundy, hunched, quiet, absorbed; Miss Gibson, straight, still, disapproving at first, then relaxing into a better companion than Annabel had expected.

"Oh, they must. They *must* do it!" gasped Miss Gibson at half-time. Her large eyes glistened. "Oh, the poor boys if they don't manage it today."

Mrs Grundy leant across Annabel to Miss Gibson.

"Don't you worry, my dear," she said. "They'll come through. They won't let my Jim down now they've come this far."

Annabel wondered whether to get up and leave them to it.

The teams were coming back on the pitch. Kevin walked next to Stu.

"God, I miss Ronnie!" said Kevin.

Stu said nothing. He felt Ronnie's presence like a ghost, an invisible substitute.

"You see if I don't score this half," said Kevin. "I'll score for him."

Again, Stu couldn't answer. He merely touched Kevin's shoulder and broke away to his place in midfield.

Then he stood, waiting for the referee's whistle. He looked round. He rubbed his eyes. I'm seeing things, he thought. For a moment it seemed as if Geoff, Ted, Ade and Ronnie were there on the field and Radwick Rangers was suddenly a team of fifteen, with the four extra urging the rest on, geeing them up for one last effort. Then they were gone. Stu looked round again. Time seemed to stand still.

As it did for Wagstaffe and Cumberland.

As it did for Annabel.

As it did for two other people somewhere within the packed confines of Wembley Stadium. Because all the main actors in the drama knew that when the referee blew his whistle, the last act would have started.

The whole crowd hushed.

Each Radwick player tensed himself, gritted his teeth, made a resolve.

Then came the shrill blast on the whistle, and life started again.

"This is more like it," said George as he and Wally sat together on the bench below the Royal Box.

There was tightness, purpose, order now in Radwick's play. And something else as well – flair. Stu's searching passes, the trickery of Gus, the speed on the wing of Nicky, the energy of Dave, the pervasive calm of Winston – it was as if Ronnie was there again giving a bit of himself to every player: a quality to use today and keep for ever as a legacy.

Radwick played themselves back into the game, absorbing and beating off the City attacks as they tried to make the game safe immediately after the restart. They began to mount attacks of their own and the pressure steadily mounted – searching, probing for a way through.

But no goals came. Stu shot wide, Gus forced a desperate save from the City goalkeeper and Dave headed against the bar. Was it all to be in vain?

Two minutes remained. Winston worked the ball away from the Radwick penalty area. His long diagonal pass found Dave, who slipped the ball to Lee, who found Stu. Stu sent Nicky away down the right and Nicky got to the goal line and crossed high into the box. Kevin was there on the six-yard line. He controlled the ball, turned and blasted it low into the net in one easy movement.

One end of the stadium was awash with red and yellow. The noise of relief, of joy, rolled round Wembley. Kevin disappeared under a tidal wave of players. Wally and George and all the substitutes leapt up and hugged each other. In the Royal Box, Walter Blyton stood and punched the air. Annabel was taken over by a deep feeling of pleasure for Stu and all the others who had gone through so much. Miss Gibson permitted herself another smile and Annabel was sure an unobtrusive tear glistened. Connie Wilshaw had gone almost demented. Meanwhile, Annabel felt her arm gripped by strong fingers. Mrs Grundy was affected as well.

Now Radwick went all out for a winner. Injury time was being played. Stu dispossessed the City number 4 and moved forward with the ball. The City defence fell back in front of him. He looked up and around. Nicky to the right, Gus to the left, Kevin up front. Stu chose deliberately. Delicately, with absolute accuracy, he delivered a high, floating ball directly to the feet of Kevin. It was worthy of Ronnie, worthy of Billy Manners when he *meant* to do things right.

Stu stopped, watched and waited for the inevitable goal. Kevin coolly trapped the ball, turned and delivered a screaming shot from twelve yards that left the City keeper groping. Stu and the rest of the Radwick team threw their arms in the air.

The ball hit the inside of the post, came out and a City defender scrambled it away. The final whistle blew. Kevin stood, head in hands. The roars of exultation from the Radwick end were suddenly stilled.

Extra time.

George and Wally rushed onto the pitch.

"Don't let that miss worry you," said Wally. "Kevin, the shot was brilliant. You can do it again and make it count."

"You've got their measure," said George. "Don't change."

Two halves of fifteen minutes each. Two teams weary and drained. A dour battle for survival. No goals. Full-time came. The match had gone to penalties.

Wembley was quiet. The tension crackled. Five penalties each, taken alternately, City first. If the scores were level after the first five, then more penalties would be taken until one team cracked.

The ball was on the spot. The City number 9 strode up. He shot low and clinically into the net. Chris Kingdon never moved.

Winston next. Just as deliberately, with impassive calmness, he turned the goalkeeper the wrong way and equalized for Rangers.

The City number 5 blasted the ball with brute strength high into the top left corner. Chris got a finger to it and spent some time wringing his hands afterwards.

Lee Boatman shot hard, straight at where the goalkeeper would have been if he hadn't guessed wrongly and dived to his right. Two-all.

The City number 11 tore in, lifted his head and sent the ball over the bar. More exultation from the Radwick end.

It was short-lived. Nicky's low shot beat the goalkeeper, clipped the post and bounced out.

Two-all still: two penalties each still to come.

The City number 7 put in a shot which Chris Kingdon got his hands to but could not prevent from going over the line.

Ossie placed the ball for Radwick's fourth attempt. The odds are on us, Stu thought. If Ossie scores, we've still got Kevin to come. Saving the best till last.

Ossie side-footed the ball almost nonchalantly into the net.

Crunch time. The last penalties of the first five coming up. Stu felt a sudden weakness at the knees. If both were converted, he'd have to take the sixth.

The City number 3 came up, put the ball carefully on the spot, turned and stepped four paces back. He turned again, made four loping strides and cracked the ball behind Chris's right shoulder into the net.

It'll be me soon, thought Stu. Kevin's bound to score.

Kevin placed the ball on the spot with equal deliberation. He stood over it for a second, staring hard at the City goalkeeper. Then he walked back six paces, stopped, pulled his socks up and adjusted the knot on his right boot.

Stu watched.

A bell rang in his mind.

He had seen this before.

Obvious. Kevin had often taken penalties.

No. Something else.

Then it poured into his mind like floodwater breaking down dams and exposing the little nugget which had lain deep under the surface detected but unrecognized.

He was watching Billy Manners taking a penalty against Burnley.

What did it mean? Billy Manners, the genius who could throw games by purposely passing to the wrong players without detection; Billy Manners, who could throw a match in which everyone thought he was a hero; Billy Manners, whose talents were so supreme that he could misuse them and no one the wiser. Except George Maxton, who knew him. And Ronnie Raikes, who was dead.

What had this to do with Kevin?

Another revelation.

No two people could move so identically if they were not intimately related.

Kevin must be Billy's son.

What did that mean? Kevin, too, was brilliant. Once in the Premiership, Kevin would be a striker for England. Wright, Cole, Sheringham, Shearer, Ferdinand, Hirst – they'd better all look out.

But could Kevin throw games undetected, like his father? Could he *mean* to hit the bar? Could he *mean* to clip a post from thirty yards?

Stu had a sudden conviction that he could.

So Kevin was playing a dirty game. But did that mean he was involved in the murders?

Of course not. He'd nearly been murdered himself.

But not quite. That could have been a put-up job.

Another realization crashed into Stu's mind.

The murders were parallel with the final stages of Radwick's promotion campaign. Radwick were *meant* to stay down.

Who by? Kevin?

Yes. Stu saw with absolute clarity what was about to happen. Kevin would take a superb penalty. It would shoot low past the despairing goalkeeper's grasping hands. It would seem destined for the far corner. But it would never reach it. The ball would clip the inside of the post. It would roll tantalizingly along the goal line but never over it. Kevin would bury his head in his hands again. Team-mates would rush to console him. "Unlucky, Kevin!" they would cry, as they had so often in the last seven games of the season.

But, inside, Kevin would be laughing because he had done his job so well.

But then again – why wait till penalties? Why did Kevin equalize when the job could have been done at ordinary time?

Kevin and whoever he worked with must be so sure of themselves. Why, they'd even *pointed* to themselves, taunted their pursuers, taunted *him*. Why else should the Billy Manners video be taken out of Ronnie's flat and put in his car right under their noses? And the delay of the result until the last penalty was for a reason. They were planning something big – a last flourish. The end of the revenge was here.

All this flashed through Stu's mind in a split second. The first inkling came as Kevin stooped to tie his lace; the resolution of what to do came as he straightened up.

Kevin turned and started his run.

Stu shouted.

"No!"

Kevin turned.

Stu ran towards him.

"What are you doing, you idiot?" yelled Kevin.

Stu bundled him out of the way with a fair shoulder charge. It had crossed his mind that he didn't know the punishment for fouling a player on your own side.

Kevin stumbled and lost his balance. Stu carried on towards the ball lying patiently on the penalty spot.

I'm committed, he thought. *I mustn't muck it up now.*

He steadied himself, saw the face of the flabbergasted City keeper twelve yards away and let fly a shot that he knew would hit the top of the net the split-second it left his boot.

Then he turned again towards Kevin.

Kevin had picked himself up. His face seemed to have collapsed, like an inflatable doll with a puncture. He was looking towards the stands and the Royal Box, as if trying to pick out a face in the crowd. Then he broke into a run towards the touchline, the bench and the Royal Box. He was shouting.

"Mum! Mum! It's gone wrong! What shall I do?"

Stu chased after him.

The referee wisely assumed that any trouble was the team's business, not his. The match – and the entire football season – had to be completed. He put the ball on the spot and motioned the City captain to get his players moving.

The City number 2 was to take the penalty. Bemused and unsettled, he shot weakly straight into Chris Kingdon's hands.

Dave Prendergast came up for Radwick's sixth. Two confident strides and the ball was in the bottom corner of the net.

Radwick Rangers had made it to the Premiership.

16

Kevin dashed sixty metres. Stu followed two seconds behind. As he ran, questions and answers flashed through his mind.

Kevin. So many things he had done were suddenly significant.

Geoff's murder. Kevin in the dressing-room, pale as a ghost. "Why Geoff?"

Why indeed? Kevin knew who it *should* have been – Ronnie. Why?

On the coach. Ronnie first mentioning Billy Manners. Who sat with him? Kevin. Ronnie speaking. "I told you a fortnight ago on the coach to Southend."

Yes, Ronnie. And you showed you knew too much. You signed your own death warrant.

But *who* did Kevin tell? Who's the other half of this deadly partnership?

A blank.

Think.

Think!

Why was Kevin taking the final penalty? The plan was that he should take the first.

Why was the plan changed?

Wally Kerns decided on Kevin first, then Winston and the rest. Kevin came out with that plausible rubbish about pressure and psychology.

And Wally said: "Good thinking, Kevin. I like it. That's what we'll do."

Too easy. Wally never even thought about it. Not like him. Was that a show put on by two conspirators?

Kevin reached the bench. George and Wally stood together, George's face suffused with fury. He stepped forward to intercept Kevin and Stu.

But Kevin wasn't to be stopped. He looked beyond George, shouting *"Mum! What shall I do?"*

Kevin's eyes registered a blurred scene. He searched for the face he wanted. Four together. Annabel (Not for him. But in another life, with other chances? Never. His way was set: his exile from what others enjoyed complete.) Connie Wilshaw, still more concerned at Radwick's victory than the new battle spawning before her eyes. Mrs Grundy, eyes cast down, avoiding his gaze. A face

of no consequence. Miss Gibson? Ah, there was a sight.
There, he saw correspondences. That tall figure, strong,
firm-jawed, with still a riot of blonde hair – yes, what
memories of a terrified childhood it brought back.

And look. Someone is coming down the steps of the
Royal Box to meet him.

So now the crisis is here and nothing is what it
seems.

Seventy thousand people had watched and gasped
as Stu barged Kevin aside. Half had roared as Stu's
shot hit the net. Few heard Kevin's cry: "Mum!
What shall I do?"

But Annabel did. For a moment, she had
thought her man had gone off his head. Then she
heard Kevin. At once she knew what Stu was
doing and why.

She wanted to meet him. She left her seat to run
down the steps from the Royal Box.

But someone was in front of her. As she reached
the gangway, Annabel collided with Mrs Grundy's
umbrella. She picked it up to throw it out of the
way, then she saw that it was open. Why?

And who was plunging down the steps ahead of
her?

Mrs Grundy, spry for so tiny and venerable a
lady.

Annabel looked back. Miss Gibson, imposing
like a Valkyrie, stared forward, unmoving.

Annabel turned again. Mrs Grundy had now traversed the steps down which so many teams had stumbled over the years. She had reached George, Wally, Kevin and Stu, still clutching her handbag. Annabel followed.

A pounding on the steps behind her meant others were about to join them.

"What in God's name is happening?" Wagstaffe had said when Stu shouldered Kevin aside.

"Maxton will have Stu for breakfast," replied Cumberland. "What does he think he's doing?"

Then they heard Kevin's high, carrying voice.

"This is it! Come on!" shouted Wagstaffe.

"Who does he mean, *Mum*?" yelled Cumberland.

"God knows," replied Wagstaffe. "But watch Kerns and Maxton."

The two men pushed past annoyed spectators and scrambled down the steps. From the surrounding crowd two plain-clothes detectives joined them. They rushed to the bench as Stu approached, shouting, "It's Wally and Kevin!"

"Get Kerns!" Wagstaffe shouted.

"I was right!" yelled Cumberland ecstatically.

The two policemen seized Wally and bundled him away.

Puzzled, George Maxton looked at Mrs Grundy.

Beyond her he saw Kevin, panting and flustered. Meanwhile, Wally was spluttering inarticulately as he was dragged away.

"What's going on?" said George.

"I'm here to protect you," said Mrs Grundy. "That Kevin, he's a bad one, he is. He means no good to you, George. And Mr Kerns as well. Who would have thought it?"

"Mum?" shouted Kevin.

The word came out as a question. His eyes travelled from Miss Gibson to Mrs Grundy and the contrast made his earlier remembrances even more bizarre.

Stu saw Annabel reach the group. He reached out and grasped her hand tightly.

"What do you mean?" said George in the patronizing voice he reserved for humble tea-ladies.

Mrs Grundy opened her handbag and produced something wrapped in a blue scarf.

"I mean this, George," she said.

Stu, Annabel, Inspector Wagstaffe and Sergeant Cumberland were witnesses to what happened next.

Dowdy Mrs Grundy grew before their eyes. Bowed shoulders straightened to a statuesque body. The slack, nondescript face peering from under wispy auburn hair strengthened, focused, found detail. Puffy cheeks deflated and spat-out cotton wool landed soggily on the ground. This new face had high cheekbones and, after a movement of jaw muscles, a firm chin. The person in front of them was a foot taller: with a final flourish she whipped off the auburn wig to reveal startling blonde hair piled on top of her head. A movement with her hand on the back of her neck, and the long yellow hair cascaded down her back.

The little knot of people by the Radwick bench who watched her could have been cast away on a desert island for all the consciousness they now had of Wembley and its seventy-thousand crowd.

Annabel spoke.

"Watch George."

He was deathly pale. He staggered as if hit. Then he recovered and stared this metamorphosis in the face.

"Irene!" he said. "Irene Manners! But you're dead."

"Does it look like it, George?" she replied.

"How could you be here, close to me for all this time, and I not know you?" George stammered.

"I was a showman's daughter, remember?" she said. "If I hadn't married Billy I could have made my name in the circus: contortionist, trapeze, high-wire, acrobatics – anything. Billy wasn't the only talented one in the family. Nor is my Kevin."

Inspector Wagstaffe collected his scattered wits.

"Irene Manners," he said, "it is my duty to—"

"No it isn't, Inspector," said Irene Manners sweetly, "and it never will be."

She passed the object wrapped in the blue scarf to Kevin.

"Don't fear to use it, son," she said. "On dear Annabel first."

Kevin removed the scarf; he held a revolver.

The gun that killed Ronnie and Ade, Stu thought.

Kevin moved quickly to Annabel and pushed the revolver into her ribs. Stu made a move to spring at him.

"I shouldn't, Stu," said Irene Manners. "He'll kill her if anyone makes a move. I've fed little Annabel with so many nice cakes that the least she can do in return is be my hostage."

"What do you want?" said Wagstaffe.

"*Him!*" said Irene, pointing at George.

All eyes followed her outstretched hand. There was something new in it: a knife, wicked, sharp, shining. A throwing knife, the same as that buried in Geoff Rundle's back.

Irene saw Stu looking at it.

"Yes, Stu," she said. "If it weren't for you, this knife would have done the business by now. My umbrella up to shield my poor old weak head, everybody groaning because my Kevin had missed his penalty and George Maxton's dreams were dust – and then a blade appears from nowhere and buries itself in his back, while a little old lady folds her umbrella up and nobody notices the wicked throw she's made. And George's last knowledge is the stench of failure. Sweet justice. But you stopped me, young Stu. So we have to think again."

The group was now surrounded by police, both uniformed and plain-clothes.

"Get them off," said Irene, "or you know what will happen to the girl."

"Stand off!" Wagstaffe shouted. "They're killers. They mean it."

"Now," said Irene, "let's move."

So the seven-strong group worked its way slowly backwards along the Royal Tunnel. Lines of shocked faces watched them. Annabel had virtually fainted with fear: Kevin's revolver was all that held her up. Half of Stu was blind with rage, the other half stayed sensible. Wagstaffe and Cumberland knew their only role now was to wait, to keep the hostages safe and trust that Irene would make a mistake.

And George? George could feel the sharpness of Irene's knife pierce his clothes and touch his skin. And the ghosts swirling round his mind presented him with certainties which rocked his being to the core.

"What do you want?" said Wagstaffe. "A get-away car? A plane abroad? It's your only chance. Can't you see that today's been a disaster?"

"Wait and see," said Irene.

They had reached the end of the Royal Tunnel and stood by the huge wooden doors, red with black beams, which closed off the outside world like the gates of a medieval fortress.

Everyone had forgotten Wally Kerns. When first bundled away, he was too shocked to speak and was hustled along the touchline as the real drama unfolded. But twenty metres away he found his voice.

"What do you think you're doing, you twerps?" he spluttered.

"We're arresting you on suspicion of murder," said a policeman.

Wally was now too angry to be shocked.

"Don't be so flaming stupid," he yelled. "I've got nothing to do with it. I'm the coach."

He looked back to the scene at the bench – the gun, the knife, the hostage-taking and Wagstaffe's voice: "*Stand off!*"

"That's where you ought to be," said Wally. "And you'll need me to help you out of the mess."

The two policemen looked at each other. Then they let go of Wally.

"Stay with us," said one.

"You bet!" said Wally.

"Now what?" said Wagstaffe. "There's nowhere to go. If you're making a deal, now's the time."

"Shut up," said Irene scornfully. "You'll not fluster me. How many times do you think I've been to Wembley Stadium? I know it better than you know your own nick."

She motioned towards the door set in the gates. "Open it," she said.

Cumberland tried. "Locked," he said.

"Unlock it," said Irene.

"Get a steward with a key," shouted Wagstaffe. "Quick!"

"Did you know," said Irene, "that these gates are modelled on Traitors' Gate at the Tower of London? So they're ideal for your last exit, eh, George?"

George's face was grey.

A moment later the door was unlocked.

"Leave it closed," said Irene. "I want a minibus or a transit van with a full tank and no following, and *no tricks*."

Wagstaffe shouted her message. The watching crowd received it in silence, except for Wally.

"Don't worry boss. We'll sort it out," he shouted.

But George was beyond hearing.

They waited. From time to time Irene Manners looked through the little spyhole on the door. At last she said, "Is that it?"

She opened the door and the group filed

through. A white ambulance stood waiting, LONDON AMBULANCE SERVICE painted on its side. Irene opened the rear door and motioned everyone in. She went to the front and held the knife to the driver's throat.

"Out," she said.

The driver looked at Wagstaffe, who nodded.

Then Irene turned to Stu. He saw a gleam of crazy logic, of psychopathic madness in her eyes.

"Drive," she said.

"How can I?" spluttered Stu. "I've still got my boots on. What about the studs?"

"Drive," she repeated. The word itself was like a knife cut.

Stu scrambled into the driving seat.

"I've not driven anything as big as this before," he said.

The radio-telephone crackled. *We won't be alone*, thought Stu. Irene wrenched it from its socket.

Stu's mind raced furiously. Why should she do that? Surely hijackers and hostage-takers would need to stay in touch so they could do deals with the police. A suspicion about what Irene intended crept into his brain and settled there like a lump of lead. With a feeling of hopelessness, he started the engine, pushed down on the clutch and engaged first gear. The ambulance jerked forward.

"Straight ahead down Olympic Way. Fast."

"But it's pedestrians only."

"Do it."

The ambulance leapt in fits and starts down the smooth concrete walkway. Supporters making for the station jumped out of the way and shook their fists. By the time they reached the end, Stu thought he had the hang of the ambulance despite his studs.

"Make for the North Circular Road," hissed Irene.

Stu desperately followed signposts until he reached the broad three-lane highway.

"Now, go north!" Irene snapped.

Do what she says, he thought. Never mind the 40 limit.

The ambulance had gone. Wally was hustled again, this time to the Event Control Centre where banks of television monitors watched the whole stadium. In Traffic Control police and Wembley staff monitored the departing cars and coaches.

A policeman spoke to Wally.

"Where will they make for?"

"Not a clue."

"Well, she must have hoped she'd bucked the system by going up Olympic Way," said someone, staring at a monitor.

"They're moving clockwise on the North Circular," said someone else.

"Right," said the policeman to Wally. "Come with me."

* * *

Stu's mind raced. If his suspicion was right, this journey with a psychopathic killer could end in death: without doubt, one false move and a bullet would be pumped into Annabel.

But he was enjoying it just a little, hurling this ambulance along the North Circular. He considered switching the siren on: he'd always wanted to make a *nee-norr, nee-norr* noise.

No, perhaps not. Keep quiet and keep listening. He made sure the connecting door between cab and rear was open and that he could keep watch through the rear-view mirror.

At first, silence. Then Wagstaffe's voice.

"Give up. You've no way out."

"Yes, there is," said Irene. "I have it planned to the last second."

"But this is a disaster."

"No. I've won. My revenge is here. All I've lived for. And when I've taken it, I don't care who else I take with me."

There was a chilled silence again. *I was right*, thought Stu.

Then George.

"I don't deserve this, Irene."

Irene's voice swelled into rage.

"You killed my Billy."

"But he's not dead. He's abroad."

"*You killed him.*"

"No. I was his friend."

"You killed him when you sent the letter."

"What letter?"

"The anonymous one to the chairman about Billy."

"You can't prove that," said Wagstaffe. "It's not in the files."

"I know," said Irene. She drew a sheet of yellowing typed paper out of her handbag. "It's here."

"Where did you get that?" said Wagstaffe.

"If I can lead you a dance for seven weeks, getting a letter out of a simple filing cabinet shouldn't be too hard."

"All right," said George. "I shopped him. But you know why, Irene. June 1970. You remember?"

Irene stiffened.

"Don't say it, George. I warn you, don't say it."

But George did. His voice rose.

"We were good together, you and me. We had everything going for us. You should have left him and come with me. You wanted to. I know it."

"*Shut up!*" screamed Irene.

"What was Billy? A loser. What could he do but play football? A weak little twerp. In debt over his head. Spineless. No guts. Gave way to temptation. What he did was terrible. It revolted me. He deserved to be shopped."

"I warned you, George," Irene shrieked.

"And you knew it. That's why you wanted me,

Irene. I was strong. I could look afer you."

Irene's voice changed. It was now ice-cold with contempt.

"Why should you think I needed looking after, George Maxton?"

"You and the boy," said George.

"What's the boy got to do with you?" said Irene.

"Everything," said George. "I see it all now. That week we spent together in Torquay when Billy was away with England in Mexico. The most wonderful time in my life. And for you, too, Irene. Believe it. That's proof."

"Proof of what?" said Irene.

"That Kevin's my son. I knew it when he was born but I couldn't say anything then. But I wasn't going to watch him grow up and not know who his father really was. So that's why I wrote the letter, Irene. To get Billy out of the way. So you and I could be together. But I'd *never* kill him. Not Billy. And then he left you and I thought . . . But you went away as well and took the boy with you and I couldn't find you."

Irene listened. Her face turned pale.

"You miserable rat, George," she said. "How *dare* you even think Kevin's your son?"

Kevin spoke, an anguished howl.

"He's *not* my dad. He's *not*. Billy is."

Through the rear-view mirror, Stu could see

George get up and go over to where Kevin sat next to Annabel still holding the revolver.

"Come on, son," said George. "We meet at last. Let's make up for lost time."

Irene made a convulsive movement. Horrified, Stu took his eyes off the road and turned to watch. Plunging towards George, she shoved the knife deep into his back, high up by the left shoulder. George slumped forward, his gurgling scream filling the ambulance.

Stu just managed to turn his head back and keep the ambulance on the road. He was still belting along the North Circular, through Edmonton and approaching the A10 roundabout – the Great Cambridge Road.

Wally was brought to the carpark and a blue Vauxhall Senator.

"Take an unmarked car," the superintendent had said. "They mustn't know we're following. They've cut off communication. I don't like it."

So now he sat next to the plain-clothes police driver, trying to make sense of his new role.

"Keep them in sight," he had been told. "You know everyone in the ambulance. You'll probably be the chief negotiator."

"Me?" Wally had gasped. He was regretting his early offer of help. "What shall I say?"

"Don't worry. We'll be with you."

So here he was, with two armed policemen in the back, feeling very strange. Crackly messages he could not make out kept coming over the radio.

"They'll make for the first motorway," said the driver.

But no. The ambulance had spurned the M1 and the A1.

"Where's that woman taking us?" muttered the driver.

Stu slowed for the roundabout.

"Straight ahead?" he shouted.

There would surely be no answer from the noisy chaos in the back.

But no: Irene was still in charge of the situation. She turned and looked at Stu with chilling calmness. Her eyes glittered.

"No," she said. "Go left at the next roundabout. Follow the road north till I say. That is where our destiny lies."

What destiny? Even when things fell to pieces around her, Irene seemed to know exactly what she wanted.

Stu took the main exit to the left and headed up the A10 towards Cambridge.

"Why should they go up there?" said the police driver.

"Search me," answered Wally.

"Let him bleed," Irene Manners shouted.

George lay face down on the floor. Blood soaked his tracksuit top. Wagstaffe and Cumberland bent over him. Cumberland, angry, looked up at Irene.

"For pity's sake, Irene. He's still alive."

"So what?" she said. "We're all going together. In my time."

"This is an ambulance," said Wagstaffe. "We can help him."

"Don't touch anything!" shrieked Irene.

"You're mad," said Cumberland. He tore off his jacket and shirt and ripped his shirt into strips. Wagstaffe pulled George's tracksuit away and exposed the deep, welling wound. Kevin watched as they bound the wound tightly with the improvized bandages. He kept up the refrain: "He's not my dad. Billy is."

Annabel shuddered and shrank within herself. Kevin had the revolver, and he was turning critical, like a nuclear reactor melting down.

The Vauxhall Senator followed as they approached the M25.

"What daft dance is this?" said the driver.

"I knew they'd make for a motorway," said the driver. "They could go anywhere now."

But no, the ambulance skidded straight over the roundabout and headed up the A10.

Stu now followed a dual carriageway past houses, through traffic lights, looking down on drivers about their business as if in another world. Through the mirror he could see George, lying face down, and Cumberland, bare to the waist, binding strips of shirt tightly round his chest. He saw Annabel still shrinking away from the dully-staring Kevin. And Inspector Wagstaffe sat facing Irene, never taking his eyes off her.

"All right," he was saying. "So you fooled us. But why? If you wanted revenge on George, why kill all the others?"

Irene laughed.

"What point would there be in just killing him? I could have done that any time in twenty years. No, I wanted to destroy his *life*, his reputation, what he stood for. He had to die at the moment of maximum humiliation: the moment his failure stared him in the face."

"But you failed," said Wagstaffe. "Radwick are promoted and now he knows he's been a father all these years. If he dies now, he dies happy. More than Geoff did, or Ted, or Ade, or Ronnie. Why them, Irene?"

"Do you read Shakespeare?" said Irene.

Wagstaffe nodded.

"Then you'll know this: 'There is a divinity that shapes our ends, rough hew them how we will.' I rough-hewed the plan: I knew my guiding star would shape the ends. I rough-hewed my plan over years and years, since the last moment I saw my Billy."

"Where is he now, Irene?" said Wagstaffe.

Irene laughed.

"You'll never know. When we're all gone, your underlings can start looking for him. Is he abroad? Has he changed his name? That's something for you to find out." She paused and looked fondly at Kevin. "But we'll never forget him, will we, my love?"

Kevin repeated, like a child, "George isn't my dad. Billy is."

"When Billy had gone," Irene went on, "I waited. Kevin wasn't called Kevin then and he didn't look like he looks now. We went away where George couldn't find us, till the time came to fake my death. Easy. Take a down-and-out off the streets, get her drunk and insensible, change her clothes for mine, douse the place with petrol and set fire to it: who'll disbelieve the grieving son who identifies me? And I disappear from sight. But don't worry, I'm around. Kevin goes away for a year or two, and then comes back from Philadelphia with a new name, a new passport and a new nose – and a football talent as great as his father's. We make sure he's spotted by George, who's Radwick's manager by now. And once Kevin's safely signed for Radwick Rangers then I go there myself."

Silence. Her hearers knew an awful revelation was at hand.

"I move around the town, I watch, I listen. I hear of a faithful supporter dying of pneumonia in a little terrace house in Kitchener Street looked after by his downtrodden, mousy wife hardly anyone ever sees. I watch them from a distance while he dies. I follow his silent wife. I stand behind her at bus stops, in supermarket checkout queues. I overhear her as she changes her library books. I know how she looks, how she moves, how she sounds, I practise her walk, her voice. I train my face to collapse so it looks like hers. And then poor Jim is gone. I stand unobserved by the graveside for the last time as myself; Mrs Grundy stands there for the last time as anybody at all."

Wagstaffe looked at her and shuddered.

"A week later, Mrs Grundy is safely under the floorboards, courtesy of me. And *I* become *her* and the idiot Blyton is taken in like a child. He generously opens the gates to the tiger and at once George Maxton is doomed."

In spite of the gun pressing in her ribs, Annabel found herself thinking of all the cakes and felt sick.

"So a new season's here: the season of my

revenge. And we bide our time till the right moment. April. Radwick top, thanks to Kevin and Ronnie and the run-in to glory starts – so the killing has to as well. Who first? Well, Ronnie blabs to Kevin. Kevin tells me all. Ronnie remembers Billy and George. I'd forgotten he was there. Ronnie can spoil things. Ronnie must go. Kevin knows Ronnie will be substituted. And he knows when. So I wait. And I do the business. But, lo and behold, it's not Ronnie. Who was to know Geoff Rundle would be sent off? And who cares? Ronnie can wait. My mistake can lead to some *real* sport. I listen to Kevin. I know about Ted and Geoff arguing. I know about Ade's fear of Geoff. So I send you a letter. You fall for it. I start a pattern of killing your main suspect as soon as you've seen him. Clever, eh?"

Wagstaffe didn't answer.

"All right, Ted and Geoff having rows over match-fixing just like Billy's was something I didn't bargain for. I knew it would start Ronnie thinking – and I wasn't prepared for George's ludicrous confession. Now everybody's talking about Billy Manners. But then, I think, why not let them? I follow Stu and the girl to Ronnie's flat. I know Ronnie's been confiding in Stu, so I make them come downstairs while I get inside. Yes, the leap from fire escape to larder window is nothing to me: I'm a showman's daughter. Stu wants to see Billy?

Well, he shall. I give him Ronnie's precious video. Much good will it do him, because Ronnie will soon be on his way out. But who's to be next, I wonder?"

"Not your own son?" said Wagstaffe.

"Oh, no," said Irene. "We were proud of that. First Kevin implicates *me*. Revenge is all people can talk about, so why not let me, little Mrs Grundy, be suspected and then passed over? And Kevin's near-death? He did that nicely, don't you think? Kevin escapes a really nasty murder attempt. Isn't he lucky? Yes, and just in time for Ronnie to go the way of all flesh and then for Stu to ring me up and *tell* me that he's rumbled what happened."

"Why did you pick up the phone?" said Wagstaffe.

"Why not? I wanted you to know I was there. Like you knew I was there every other time. Like a ghost, a sprite, a Jack o' Lantern. Little Mrs Grundy, so invisible that nobody noticed when she wasn't there because hardly anyone knew when she was! What a partnership we were, Kevin and me! Over the end of the season, our strike rate was better than Kevin and Ronnie's at the start."

"But you can't have worked out what would happen today?"

"Yes, I could. Well enough to take chances as they came up. Kevin could have lost the match in ordinary time, but no. Why not go for broke, for the big effect, for complete control? Penalties, with everything depending on Kevin's? Keep the agony up. Kevin could do it. Kevin can do *anything he likes* on a football field. And it should have worked. Kevin would miss and George would fail and die all in the same moment. Little Mrs Grundy would disappear in the mayhem, gone for ever. Kevin would be distraught and ask for a transfer next season. Nothing more would happen. The files would be closed on one of the great unsolved crimes. If it hadn't been for young Stu. Another reason for Stu not to see the day out alive."

Stu heard that, but his hands on the steering wheel never shook. He knew that in this game his nerve mustn't falter. The tableau of people in the back of the ambulance stayed immobile, like some nightmarish painting. All the time he saw Annabel's face, frozen into terror.

He drove along a wide dual carriageway deep into the countryside, passing turn-offs for Hoddesdon, Harlow, Chelmsford, Ware. He kept on. At this rate I can visit my auntie in Buntingford, he thought. He passed a junction for Hertford, and then the shallow cutting through which the road disappeared. They were on a long bridge and far below them was the valley of the River Lea.

Irene saw. She turned to Stu.

"*Stop!*" she shrieked. "This is the place."

Stu hit the brakes hard. The ambulance slewed

to one side and came to a halt against the safety fence. Stu switched the hazard warning lights on and sat immobile. Suddenly, it was very quiet.

"Out!" said Irene. "All of you."

Wagstaffe opened the doors at the back. Kevin stood and, revolver at the ready, motioned Annabel and Wagstaffe out.

"You too," Irene shouted to Cumberland.

"What about George?"

"Leave him."

At that moment, George's body arched convulsively and he gave a long, shuddering moan. Then he was still. Cumberland bent, listened and felt his wrist. He rose slowly.

"He's dead. You've killed him."

"He won't be the last today," replied Irene.

Wagstaffe smiled grimly.

"Like I said before," he murmured, "Radwick promoted and knowledge of a new son – George died happy. Funny sort of revenge."

"Shut up!" Irene screamed.

Kevin was moaning again. "George isn't my dad. Billy is."

Irene seemed proof against distraction. "Line up against the fence," she said.

They did so. Below them, a railway line gleamed in the evening sun, cows and horses grazed peacefully, a canalized river flowed softly and at the far side of the bridge a narrow-boat chugged up the

River Lea itself. The line of people stood with their backs to the fence. Irene Manners put the knife in her handbag and brought out a second revolver. On the end of the barrel was a stubby silencer.

"Turn round," she commanded.

Stu looked at the idyllic scene in front of him and knew he was right. He had seen the madness in her eyes. Irene was resolved that none of them would see the end of the day alive, and this was the place of execution.

He heard a click. Irene was ready to use the gun. Out of the corner of his eye Stu could see Kevin still threateningly close to Annabel.

A sick feeling enveloped him.

I'm in front of a firing squad. This is the last sight we shall ever see. She really does mean to take us all with her.

For this place was their destiny. A fence to line up against; a drop below for bodies to fall; perilously few cars passing whose drivers might think, Strange. What's going on there? He and the others waited.

But surely we can do *something*, thought Stu. Hasn't it occurred to anyone else what she intends? She can't just *do* this, can she?

My God, she can! She will. What can stop her?

What if I shout out: "*She's going to kill us all*"?

Then it will start. Kevin will shoot Annabel,

and then what? One by one: Stu, Wagstaffe, Cumberland. So Irene and Kevin will be left. And then?

What had Irene said? *"I don't care who I take with me."* And later: *"We're all going together."*

So Irene included herself in this. And she and Kevin had decided on a suicide pact. Had they? When?

If they had, it must have been today, after the plan had gone wrong. But what chance had there been for that?

No. It couldn't be. Kevin wasn't going to consent meekly to die. Was he?

Stu made his mind up. For the second time that day, Kevin was the weak link. He wasn't party to Irene's new plan. So what could Stu lose? If he was wrong he'd die with the rest anyway. If he was right . . .

He shouted at the top of his voice.

"Kevin! She means you as well."

He waited for Kevin to shout "No use, Stu!" and the shot that would kill Annabel.

It never came. Kevin's face, dull, tranced, turned towards him. Then the unnatural quiet was shattered. The Vauxhall Senator had pulled up unnoticed fifty metres away, wails of police sirens came from all sides and within a few minutes the bridge was sealed off at both ends.

A voice reached them through a loud-hailer.

"Irene Manners, you are surrounded by armed police. Resistance to arrest is useless. Throw down your weapons and give yourself up."

Irene shrieked back. Stu turned round and once again saw madness glittering in her eyes.

"Never! Everyone here is going to die, including me. And I'll take some of you with me."

"She's barmy," muttered the driver to Wally.

"Ten seconds!" shouted Irene. "Get your people off in ten seconds or the girl dies first. One . . ."

Nobody moved.

"Two . . ."

A group of police were talking among themselves, casting covert looks at Wally.

"Three . . ."

The superintendent walked to him and spoke.

"It's time for you to do something, Wally."

"Four . . ."

Wally gulped. "What?" he said.

"Negotiate. You know these people. Someone may listen to you."

"Fat chance!" said Wally.

"Five . . ."

Quaking, Wally walked towards the group on the bridge.

"Listen," he shouted, "I don't know what you've done to George, but save the rest. Annabel, Stu, Kevin – they mustn't die."

"Six. Give me one reason why."

"Because Kevin will play for England. He'll be the greatest striker ever known."

"Seven. What's that to me?"

"You wouldn't take that away from your own son, would you?"

Kevin spoke: the same refrain. "George isn't my dad. Billy is."

"Eight." The voice was quieter, less assured.

Kevin seemed to jerk out of his trance.

"That's right, isn't it, Mum? Billy *is* my father? Not George? I couldn't stand that."

"Nine." Irene stared at her son.

"And you aren't going to kill me along with the rest, are you? That wasn't part of the bargain, was it, Mum?"

He listened to me, thought Stu.

Irene never said "ten".

Where the railway passed under the bridge was a steel barrier higher by some feet than the safety fence. Irene dropped her gun, dashed to it and vaulted with supreme grace to the top. For a moment she stood there, perfectly balanced.

"I never lied to you, Kevin," she shouted.

And then she was gone, plummeting to the tracks below.

A train rumbled along towards Liverpool Street. ·

Kevin dropped his gun. Annabel dashed to Stu and they clung to each other.

"Whatever you do, don't look over," said Stu.

George's body was removed on a stretcher. Wally stood motionless, watching it. Uniformed police dashed up to Wagstaffe and Cumberland: there was much handshaking and clapping of shoulders.

Stu and Annabel stayed in a close embrace. Kevin, the revolver on the ground by his side, sat slumped against the safety fence.

"Play for England?" a policeman muttered to Wally. "By the time he comes out he'll be too old to manage England."

Two policemen strode towards Kevin. Before they reached him, he cried out again: "George isn't my dad, Billy is. Mum said she never lied to me."

Annabel disengaged herself from Stu for a moment. She bent to Kevin and touched his shoulder.

"No," she said. "Irene didn't lie. Billy's your father. We've seen a video."

To Kevin, her form seemed dim and her voice miles away. But he heard – and knew, with an internal sob of relief, that what she said was true.

Beyond her, the policemen were coming to get him. Time slowed: they were frozen motionless as other scenes, from twenty years back, appeared in his sight.

The little boy watched as his mother fetched a stepladder and a knife. She set the ladder up by the hanging body and climbed six rungs. With infinite care she held the body under the shoulders, then cut the rope. Then, with tenderness as well as strength, she carried the body to the ground and laid it out.

She knelt down, cradled the head in her arms and – at last – cried aloud: "Billy! Oh, my Billy!"

The little boy watched and then cried himself. He was not sure what had happened, except that it was clear his daddy would not be playing with him any more.

At last the crying was done. Mummy stood up, again the strong, dependable figure who did everything right.

"You must be a big boy now," she said, "and always do what I say."

She went into the garden shed and came out with a spade.

"Watch Mummy," she said.

Then she dug. He watched for hours – dig, dig, dig until piles of earth hid her as she disappeared into a trench four feet deep, two feet wide and over six feet long.

At last she stopped.

"Say goodbye to Daddy now," she said.

She left him while he did so. She went into the house and came back with the best duvet and cover which had always been spread over Mummy and Daddy's bed.

"He mustn't feel cold," she said.

She wrapped Daddy in the duvet, then gently eased him into the trench.

The boy watched, fascinated.

She filled the trench with earth, stamped it down and then replaced the grass turves she had carefully kept to one side.

Finally, she bent down again to the little boy.

"Do you know whose fault this is?" she said.

"No, Mummy."

"Uncle George's. He's taken your Daddy away. And one day we're going to take him away, you and I together."

"Yes, Mummy."

"Nobody knows where Daddy is except us. Nobody ever will. They will think Daddy has gone away because he doesn't love us any more. But we know and we'll keep it a secret."

"Yes, Mummy." It seemed right.

She gripped his arms and stared him in the face.

"Daddy's still here with us. Always. We'll never see him but he'll be there. And he'll tell us what to do. I'll know what he wants and I'll tell you. And you'll do what I say, because you'll be doing what Daddy says. Do you see?"

"Yes, Mummy."

Her eyes bore so insistently into him that he started to cry.

"We'll take a long time to pay Uncle George back. We must wait until you're a really big boy. But then we'll do nothing else. And when we've finished, there'll be nothing else for us to do. We'll be happy and free."

"Yes, Mummy," said the little boy, through his hot and raging tears.

The scene faded: he was back on the bridge. He remembered every word and over the years had understood them. And now, *"There's nothing else for us to do."* That's true. *"We will be happy and free."* How? *"I never lied to you."* Her last words.

I do as she says. She knows how to be happy and free. Like Daddy. That's why she did what she did.

The policemen were close, their boots curving through the air with paralyzing slowness. Between them and his hand the gun still lay on the ground.

He knew now what his mother meant. He reached forward, grabbed the gun before the policemen could stop him and pressed it to his head.

A brand new series coming from Point...

Encounter worlds where men and women make hazardous voyages through space; where time travel is a reality and the fifth dimension a possibility; where the ultimate horror has already happened and mankind breaks through the barrier of technology...

Obernewtyn
Isobelle Carmody
A new breed of humans are born into a hostile world struggling back from the brink of apocalypse...

Random Factor
Jessica Palmer
Battle rages in space. War has been erased from earth and is now controlled by an all-powerful computer – until a random factor enters the system...

First Contact
Nigel Robinson
In 1992 mankind launched the search for extra-terrestial intelligence. Two hundred years later, someone responded...

Read Point SF and enter a new dimension...

The Waitress
by Sinclair Smith

The Phantom
by Barbara Steiner

The Baby-sitter
The Baby-sitter II
Beach House
Beach Party
The Boyfriend
The Dead Girlfriend
The Girlfriend
The Hitchhiker
Hit and Run
The Snowman
by R.L. Stine

Thirteen
by Christopher Pike, R.L. Stine and others

Thirteen More Tales of Horror
by Diane Hoh and others

Point Romance

Caroline B. Cooney

The lives, loves and hopes of five young girls appear in a dazzling new mini series:

Anne – coming to terms with a terrible secret that has changed her whole life.

Kip – everyone's best friend, but no one's dream date...why can't she find the right guy?

Molly – out for revenge against the four girls she has always been jealous of...

Emily – whose secure and happy life is about to be threatened by disaster.

Beth Rose – dreaming of love but wondering if it will ever become a reality.

Follow the five through their last years of high school, in four brilliant titles: *Saturday Night, Last Dance, New Year's Eve,* and *Summer Nights*

Point R♥mance

If you like Point Horror, you'll love Point Romance!

Anyone can hear the language of love.

Are you burning with passion, and aching with desire? Then these are the books for you! Point Romance brings you passion, romance, heartache . . . and *love*.

Available now:

Two Weeks in Paradise
Denise Colby

Saturday Night
Last Dance
New Year's Eve
Caroline B. Cooney

Cradle Snatcher
Alison Creaghan

Summer Dreams, Winter Love
Mary Francis Shura

The Last Great Summer
Carol Stanley

Lifeguards:
Summer's Promise
Summer's End
Todd Strasser

French Kiss
Robyn Turner

Look out for:

Summer Nights
Caroline B. Cooney

First Comes Love:
To Have and to Hold
For Better, For Worse
Jennifer Baker

Kiss Me, Stupid
Alison Creaghan

First Comes Love:
In Sickness and in Health
Jennifer Baker

A Winter Love Story
Jane Claypool Miner

Point

Pointing the way forward

More compelling reading from top authors.

The Highest Form of Killing
Malcolm Rose
Death is in the very air . . .

Seventeenth Summer
K.M. Peyton
*Patrick Pennington – mean, moody and out
of control . . .*

Secret Lives
William Taylor
*Two people drawn together by their mysterious
pasts . . .*

Flight 116 is Down
Caroline B. Cooney
Countdown to disaster . . .

Forbidden
Caroline B. Cooney
Theirs was a love that could never be . . .

Hostilities
Caroline Macdonald
*In which the everyday throws shadows of another,
more mysterious world . . .*

POINT FANTASY

Read Point Fantasy and escape into the
realms of the imagination; the kingdoms
of mortal and immortal elements. Lose
yourself in the world of the dragon and
the dark lord, the princess and the mage;
a world where magic rules and the forces
of evil are ever poised to attack . . .

Available now:

Doom Sword
Peter Beere
Adam discovers the Doom Sword and has to
face a perilous quest . . .

Brog The Stoop
Joe Boyle
Can Brog restore the Source of Light to
Drabwurld?

. **The "Renegades" series:**
Book 1: Healer's Quest
Book 2: Fire Wars
Jessica Palmer
Journey with Zelia and Ares as they combine
their magical powers to battle against evil and
restore order to their land . . .

Daine the Hunter:
Book 1: Wild Magic
Book 2: Wolf Speaker
Tamora Pierce
Follow the adventures of Daine the hunter,
who is possessed of a strange and incredible
"wild magic" . . .

POINT FANTASY

Foiling the Dragon
Susan Price
What will become of Paul Welsh, pub poet,
when he meets a dragon – with a passion for
poetry, and an appetite for poets . . .

Dragonsbane
Patricia C. Wrede
Princess Cimorene discovers that living with a
dragon is not always easy, and there is a
serious threat at hand . . .

The Webbed Hand
Jenny Jones
Princess Maria is Soprafini's only hope
against the evil Prince Ferrian and his
monstrous Fireflies . . .

Look out for:
**Daine the Hunter:
Book 3: The Emperor Mage**
Tamora Price

Star Warriors
Peter Beere

**The "Renegades" Series
Book 3: The Return of the Wizard**
Jessica Palmer

Elf-King
Susan Price

THE UNDERWORLD TRILOGY
Peter Beere

When life became impossible for the homeless of London many left the streets to live beneath the earth. They made their homes in the corridors and caves of the Underground. They gave their home a name. They called it UNDERWORLD.

UNDERWORLD
It was hard for Sarah to remember how long she'd been down there, but it sometimes seemed like forever. It was hard to remember a life on the outside. It was hard to remember the real world. Now it seemed that there was nothing but creeping on through the darkness, there was nothing but whispering and secrecy.

And in the darkness lay a man who was waiting to kill her . . .

UNDERWORLD II
"Tracey," she called quietly. No one answered. There was only the dark threatening void which forms Underworld. It's a place people can get lost in, people can disappear in. It's not a place for young girls whose big sisters have deserted them. Mandy didn't know what to do. She didn't know what had swept her sister and her friends from Underworld. All she knew was that Tracey had gone off and left her on her own.

UNDERWORLD III
Whose idea was it? Emma didn't know and now it didn't matter anyway. It was probably Adam who had said, "Let's go down and look round the Underground." It was something to tell their friends about, something new to try. To boast that they had been inside the secret Underworld, a place no one talked about, but everyone knew was there.

It had all seemed like a great adventure, until they found the gun . . .

Also by Peter Beere

CROSSFIRE
When Maggie runs away from Ireland, she finds herself roaming the streets of London destitute and alone. But Maggie has more to fear then the life of a runaway. Her step-father is an important member of the IRA – and if he doesn't find her before his enemies do, Maggie might just find herself caught up in the crossfire . . .